BROADVIEW PUBLIC LIBRARY DISTRICT
2226 S. 16th AVENUE
BROADVIEW, IL 60153
(708) 345-1325

COUNTRY STUDIES

STEVE BRACE
Series Editor: John Hopkin

Heinemann Library
Des Plaines, Illinois

1999 Reed Educational & Professional Publishing
Published by Heinemann Library,
an imprint of Reed Educational & Professional Publishing,
1350 East Touhy Avenue, Suite 240 West
Des Plaines, IL 60018

All rights reserved. No part of this publication may be reproduced or transmitted in any form or by any means, electronic or mechanical, including photocopying, recording, taping, or any information storage and retrieval system, without permission in writing from the publisher.

© Steve Brace

03 02 01 00 99
10 9 8 7 6 5 4 3 2 1

Printed in Hong Kong

Library of Congress Cataloging-in-Publication Data

Brace, Steve.
   India / Steve Brace.
     p. cm. – (Country studies)
   Includes bibliographical references and index.
   Summary: Describes the history, geography, population, economic development, natural resources, and future of India.
   ISBN 1-57572-893-1 (library binding)
   1. India—Juvenile literature. [1. India.} I. Title.
II. Series: Country studies (Des Plaines, Ill.)
DS407.B68   1999
954—dc21   98-52758
                                                              CIP
                                                              AC

Acknowledgments
The publisher would like to thank the following for permission to reproduce copyright material.
Maps and extracts
p.5 *India Year Book,* 1995; **p.6** Salil Shetty, ACTIONAID—India; **p.6** *Lonely Planet Guide to India;* **p.6** *Daily Mail,* 7 September 1995; **p.7** extract adapted from *Understanding Global Issues 97/1;* **p.10** *Lonely Planet Guide to India;* **p.14** Dr. Lohiya from Manavlok, an Indian development charity; **p.16** *India Year Book;* **p.17** *The Economist,* 1997; **p.23** *The Independent,* March 19, 1995; **p.24** *Lonely Planet Guide to India;* **p.26** data from *The Economist;* **p.28** *Financial Times;* **p.29** *The Economist,* 1997; **p.30** Kanwar Sain, chief engineer of the Indira Gandhi Canal; **p.36** 1994 World Bank Development Report; **p.36** extracts adapted from *The Financial Times,* November 8, 1994 and *Understanding Global Issues;* **p.41** *International Herald Tribune;* **p.43** *Global Eye,* Issue 4 Autumn 1997; **p.43** Philip D'Souza of *The New Internationalist;* **p.45** Clive Anderson, BBC film, *Our Man in Goa;* **p.45** cartoon from Tourism Concern; **p.45** Tourism Concern; **p.46** *The Economist;* **p.47** *The New Internationalist;* **p.49** Adapted from *The New Internationalist* and *Understanding Global Issues;* **p.51** United Nations Industrial Development Organization; **p.53** Binu S. Thomas, ACTIONAID—India; **p.55** *The Daily Telegraph,* September 10, 1997; **p.57** *Financial Times,* September 6, 1995; **p.57** The Indian Center for Science and Environment; **p.57** *The Economist,* 1997; **p.58** *The Economist.*
Photos
p.4 (bottom) Robert Harding Picture Library; **p.4 (top)** Nigel Hicks; **p.5** C Science Photo Library; **p.6 (left)** ACTIONAID; **p.6 (right)** Hutchison Library; **p.7** Hutchison Library; **p.8** British Library; **p.9 (left)** British Library; **p.9 (right)** Victoria and Albert Museum; **p.10 (left)** Panos Pictures; **p.10 (right)** ACTIONAID; **p.12 (top)** Hutchison Library; **p.12 (bottom)** Kumar-Unep/Still Pictures; **p.14** ACTIONAID; **p.16** Panos Pictures; **p.20** Images of India Picture Library; **p.22 (left)** Dinodia Picture Library; **p.22 (right)** Panos Pictures; **p.24** ACTIONAID; **p.26** ZUL; **p.27** Robert Harding Picture Library; **p.28 (left)** Panos Pictures; **p.28 (right)** Dinodia Picture Library; **p.29** Images of India Picture Library; **p.30** ImageBank; **p.31** Still Pictures; **p.32** Still Pictures; **p.33** ACTIONAID; **p.34 (left)** Still Pictures; **p.34 (right)** ACTIONAID; **p.37 (left)** ACTIONAID; **p.37 (right)** Images of India Picture Library; **p.38** Images of India Picture Library; **p.39** Hulton-Deutsch Collection; **p.40** AP/Agit Kumar; **p.41** Associated Press; **p.42 (top)** Dinodia Picture Library; **p.42 (bottom)** Dinodia Picture Library; **p.44** Images of India Picture Library; **p.48 (left)** Images of India Picture Library; **p.48 (right)** ACTIONAID; **p.50 (top)** Images of India Picture Library; **p.50 (bottom)** Ann and Bury Peerless; **p.52** Still Pictures; **p.54** Still Pictures; **p.56** Hulton Getty Picture Library; **p.57** Hutchison Library; **p.58** Robert Harding Picture Library; **p.59** Images of India Picture Library.

The publishers have made every effort to trace the copyright holders. However if any material has been overlooked or incorrectly acknowledged, we would be pleased to correct this at the earliest opportunity.

Contents

1 Introducing India — 4

India's Landscapes — 4
India's People — 6
Historical Changes — 8
India's Climate — 10
The Ganges River Basin — 12
INVESTIGATION: Earthquakes — 14

2 Population Change and Urbanization — 16

Population Structure and Growth — 16
Population and Development — 18
Urbanization and Migration — 20
Life in India's Cities — 22
INVESTIGATION: Bangalore — 24

3 Rural Development — 26

Rural India — 26
The Green Revolution — 28
Agricultural Development in the Thar Desert — 30
Small-Scale Farming in the Nilgiri Hills — 32
INVESTIGATION: Tea Plantations — 34

4 Development and Economic Growth — 36

Development in India — 36
India's Industries — 38
International Companies in India — 40
INVESTIGATION: Economic Growth in Bangalore — 42
INVESTIGATION: Tourism in Goa — 44

5 Regional and National Development — 46

Regional Inequalities in India — 46
People Involved in India's Development — 48
India's Changing Economy — 50
Development Trends in India — 52

6 India's Future — 54

India and the Global Community — 54
The Prospects for India's Development — 56
India's Future — 58

Map of India — 60
More Books to Read — 61
Glossary — 61
Index — 63

1 INTRODUCING INDIA

India's Landscapes

▶ India has a varied landscape.
▶ The land varies from low coastline to high mountains.

India's physical geography

India's landscape can be divided into a number of different areas. Along India's northern border are the Himalaya Mountains. The highest point in India is Kanchenjunga, (along the India-Nepal border) at 28,208 feet. The world's highest mountain, Mt. Everest (29,028 feet), is also in the Himalayas, but is in Nepal. To the south of these mountains are the wide, fertile plains of the Ganges Valley. In the west is the Thar Desert. Across central and southern India is the Deccan Plateau, an area of flat land about 3,200 feet high. It is bordered by the highlands of the Eastern and Western Ghats.

India also has contrasting environmental regions. The Thar Desert receives less than 12 inches of rainfall a year. Cherrapunji, in the state of Meghalaya, is one of the rainiest places in the world. It receives about 457 inches a year.

Wide river valleys and flat low-lying lands are found across the Bay of Bengal.

The Ganges River drains into the Bay of Bengal 500 miles south of the heights of the Himalayas. The river creates a huge, flat delta, where thousands of acres of land are only a few inches above sea level.

This photograph of Bhagirathi Parbat shows the high peaks and glaciers of the Indian Himalayas.

Introducing India

This satellite image shows the Indian subcontinent.

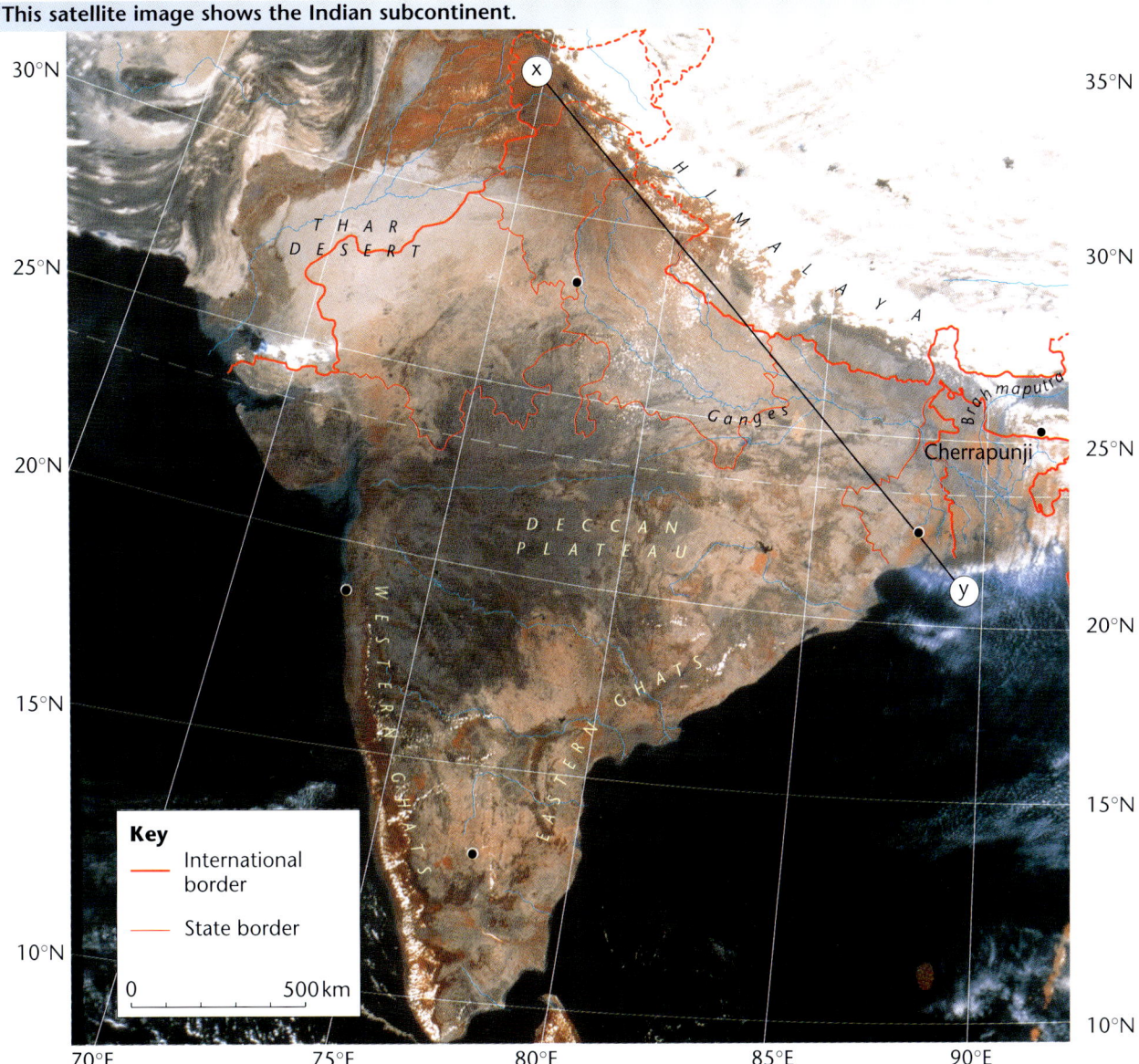

FACT FILE

Deserts, deltas, mountains, and plains

The borders of four contrasting regions—desert, delta, mountain, and plain—have been added to the satellite image above. Rajasthan lies in the northwest of India and borders Pakistan. It is largely desert. The Thar Desert stretches across hundreds of miles. West Bengal lies in the Ganges Delta. Its lands are fertile, and it is one of the most populated regions. Jammu and Kashmir is a state or region in the Himalaya Mountains. It borders China. Farming is almost impossible there. Uttar Pradesh lies in the center of northern India in fertile lowlands. The Ganges River flows through it. The land is flat and ideal for farming.

"India occupies a strategic position in Asia, looking across the seas to Arabia and Africa on the west and to Burma [now known as Myanmar], Malaysia, and the Indonesian archipelago on the east. Geographically, the Himalayan ranges kept India apart from the rest of Asia. The fertility of the Indo-Gangetic belt, however, has proved to be such an irresistible magnet that hordes of people have pressed into India through the mountain passes from ancient times. India has a land frontier of 15,200km (9,440 mi.) and a coastline of 7,516km (4,667 mi.). All the major land forms—hills, mountains, plateaus, and plains—are well-represented in India."

India Year Book, 1995

India's People

▶ **India has a diverse human geography.**

India's diverse people

"India is the world's ninth most industrialized country, with the scientific power to launch its own satellites. Its 200 million middle classes would be the envy of any developing country. India has the potential to become an economic tiger, but it is also one of the world's poorest nations."

Salil Shetty, ACTIONAID-India

"India captures the imagination. From Rajasthan's deserts to the Himalayas, from holy cows to Bengal tigers—India's extraordinary diversity fascinates travelers."

Lonely Planet Guide to India

Sampangi, one of Bangalore's many ragpickers, collects waste paper and plastic to be sold for recycling.

People sometimes describe India as a "developing" country, focusing on images of poverty. People also think of India as the source of products like tea, spices, or cotton, or as being famous for the exotic Taj Mahal. But India has a great wealth of natural and human resources. In fact there is as much diversity in this one country as you would find across all of North America.

A Calcutta family, part of India's middle class population of 200 million, enjoys a meal together.

Languages: There are 1,652 Indian "mother tongue languages." Thirty-three of these languages are each spoken by more than one million people. Hindi is the official language and English is widely spoken.

Wealth: India's **Gross Domestic Product (GDP)** per capita is $1,500 per person per year, compared to $27,607 in the United States. GDP measures the average amount of goods and services created by each person within a nation's borders. Not everyone has the same amount of money, and India's population includes both the very rich and people who live on 30 cents a day.

Religions: The many religions in India include Hinduism, Islam, Buddhism, and Sikhism. There are also Christians, Jains, and Adivasis. Most Indians are Hindus, which has a religious system called **castes**. By birth, a person is a member of one of the many castes that are arranged in a social and employment hierarchy. Discrimination based on caste was made illegal in 1947.

Guests Gather for $2.5 Million Wedding Feast
"By comparison, even royal weddings look paltry—the guest list runs to 300,000. This $2.5 million extravagance is being put on by Jayalalitha Jauaram, former film star and chief minister of Tamil Nadu."

Daily Mail September 7, 1995

Introducing India

People are gathering for the festival of Holi in Ahore, Rajasthan.

Gender: Indira Gandhi, who was twice India's Prime Minister (1966–1977 and 1980–1984), shows how women can rise to the highest levels of society. However, despite her achievements, there remains a gap between the quality of life of Indian men and women. For example, 64 percent of men can read and write, but only 36 percent of women can.

Religion	% of population
Hindu	83
Muslim	11
Christian	2.5
Sikh	2.5
Buddhist	1

India's Main Religions

FACT FILE

Hinduism and the system

Hinduism is partly a religion and partly a social system. The three most important gods are Brahma, Vishnu, and Shiva, although thousands of other gods are also worshiped. Hindus have two basic beliefs: *reincarnation* (believers come back in a different life) and *dharma*, a belief in natural laws and religious and personal duty.

India has 800 million Hindus: 23 percent belong to the upper castes, 57 percent are in the backward castes, 20 percent are untouchables, and at the top are the Brahmins (priests), the Kshatriyas (landowners), and Vaishyas (merchants). This ancient caste system had strict rules about how society was organized and how different groups should behave. For example, food cooked or touched by a member of a lower caste was thought by a member of an upper caste to be unclean.

Today the caste system is changing rapidly, especially in cities and among educated people. The 150 million untouchables are now known as Dalits (the downtrodden). Along with the backward castes, they are now an important political force, challenging the power of the upper castes.

Adapted from *Understanding Global Issues*, 1997

Historical Changes

▶ The India of today has been affected by historical changes.

Out of the past

Lady Florence Streatfield (seated left) and Sir Benjamin Simpson (standing right) enjoy a Victorian tea party in colonial Calcutta in 1890.

Ancient India

Modern India has only existed since independence in 1947. However, throughout history India has been influenced by contact with people from across Asia and Europe. This has helped to make India a varied place today. Some key events in the past were
- 2600–1600 B.C. the Indus Valley civilization built the great cities of Moenjodaro and Harappa in the Punjab.
- around 1500 B.C. the Aryan people invaded India from the North. In southern India a number of empires grew and collapsed.
- 1500–1700 A.D. the Mogul empires grew, causing India to be more like a single country.
- from around 1500 A.D. traders from Europe arrived in India by sea. They were interested in taking India's spices, rice, silk, and sugar cane back to Europe.

The British in India

India's wealth made it very attractive to the British. After 1750, Britain used force to take over the country and made it a **colony**. Britain gained control in several ways.
- The British army defeated the Indian army in battle.
- The British took control of most of India's trade.
- The British made Indians pay taxes and pay rent to landowners.
- The British set up industries in India.

Introducing India

British rule brought some benefits to India, for example:
- A national railroad system was built to help **export** goods.
- English was introduced across India and although it was foreign, it provided a common language.
- A national education system and civil service was set up.
- Export crops were introduced, such as tea, coffee, and indigo—a crop used to make blue dye.

But the British gained most from colonialism at India's expense. For example, factory owners in Britain pressured their government to put a 30 percent import tax on Indian cloth. This destroyed the cloth industry in India and allowed British factories to export cloth there.

Women workers in Bengal sort out indigo, one of the new crops introduced by the British.

Siraj-ud-Daula was the ruler of Bengal in the 1750's. He fought against the British in their attempts to take control of this area.

Robert Clive, head of the East India Company, made a fortune of $152 million. At the same time, most Indians suffered great hardships. For example, farmers in Bengal were forced to grow indigo on their land instead of food. Although 10 million people died in the Bengal famine in 1770, farmers were still forced to pay the land tax.

These sort of inequalities caused discontent in India. This discontent led the Indian people to struggle for independence. As a result of this pressure, the British withdrew from power in India, and it became independent in 1947.

FACT FILE

Gandhi (1869–1948)

Mohandas Gandhi was one of the leading figures in the struggle for Indian independence. After studying law in Britain and fighting for Indian rights in South Africa, he returned to India where he took up the cause of Indian independence. Gandhi argued that, "you have been taught that . . . British rule in India is beneficial. Nothing is more false! You cannot escape two facts: First, that under the British, India has become the world's poorest country; and second, that it is denied advantages and decencies to which any free country is entitled."

Gandhi believed in nonviolent resistance (satyagraha) to the colonialists, although other people within the independence struggle took up arms against the British. Gandhi encouraged Indians to protest in a variety of ways including not paying taxes to the British or buying British-made goods. As a result, he was imprisoned on numerous occasions. He also campaigned against the harsh treatment of low-caste members of Indian society and promoted small craft industries. Because of his actions, he became known as Mahatma or "great soul."

India's Climate

▶ India has a variety of climates.

India's tropical location

India's location close to the Equator and straddling the Tropic of Cancer means that the sun is overhead for most of the year, so temperatures are high. But there are big differences between north and south India, and between places at different **altitudes**.

> "Whilst the heat is building up to breaking point in the south, the people of Ladakh (in the north) are still waiting for the snow to melt."
>
> Lonely Planet Guide to India

The Himalayas' altitude means they have large areas of snow and ice. Here the difference between day and night temperatures can range from below freezing to 85°F.

The monsoon

India has a **monsoon** climate—named after the heavy summer rains. There are three general seasons:

- March–May: hot season. Temperatures can reach 100°F, but rainfall is often less than 1/2 inch a month.

- June–September: monsoon season. Heavy rains are brought by the moist southwest monsoon winds. The rains can last four months. Temperatures drop to around 85°F when the rains start.

- October–February: cool season. Temperatures fall to around 70°F with little rain.

The monsoon rains do not fall evenly from year to year, and there are big differences across India. The wettest areas are the upland areas, especially the Himalayas and Western Ghats. The driest areas are northwest and central India.

India has invested in **high-tech** satellite technology to help predict the start of monsoon rains. In addition, people's local knowledge of signs, such as bird migrations and changes in wind direction and speed, are also helpful.

Heavy monsoon rains fall from June to September.

The flooding of the Ganges River, following the monsoon rains, deposits a layer of fertile silt on the fields.

Introducing India

How does the monsoon affect the lives of people?

The monsoon is vitally important to India. Two-thirds of farmers rely on monsoon rainfall to water their crops. Monsoon rains make some of India's rivers rise and flood, leaving fertile silt on the surrounding flood plains. A good monsoon means better crops and more jobs in farming and farm industries. Greater use of irrigation has provided water security for some farmers, but in some places too much water has been **extracted** from aquifers, or water-bearing rocks, causing the **water table** to be lowered. The United Nations reported that this **ground water** is currently being extracted faster than it is **recharged**.

Table of Climate Data for Jaisalmer

	Max temp (°F)	Rainfall (in.)
January	75	.08
February	82	.04
March	90	.12
April	100	.08
May	108	.20
June	106	.30
July	100	3.60
August	97	3.40
September	97	.50
October	97	.04
November	88	.20
December	79	.08

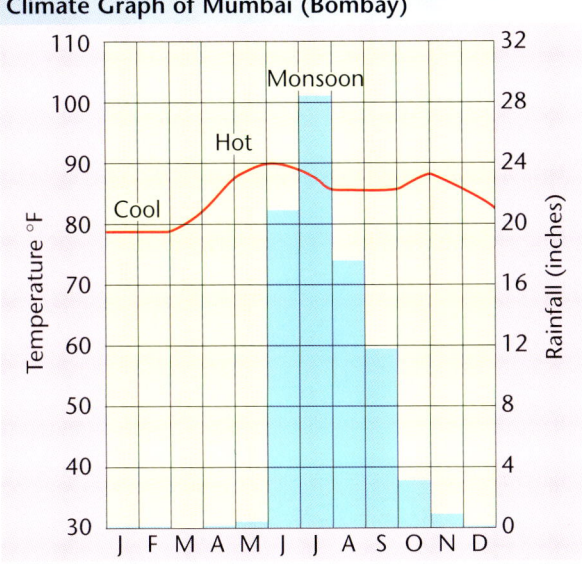

Climate Graph of Mumbai (Bombay)

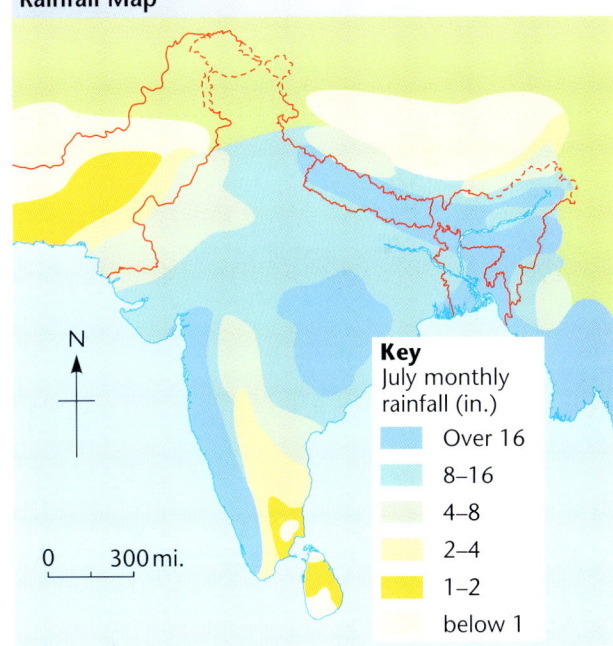

Rainfall Map

Key: July monthly rainfall (in.) — Over 16, 8–16, 4–8, 2–4, 1–2, below 1

FACT FILE

Monsoons and cyclones

Monsoon comes from the Arabic *mausin* which means seasonal wind. Over India there are two monsoon winds. In summer, southwest winds blow toward low pressure in Central Asia, bringing warm moist air and heavy rain over India. In autumn, the wind direction changes to northeast. The northeast monsoon is weaker than the summer monsoon, but farmers in east India still rely on it as their main source of water for the year. From October to December the northeast monsoon passes over India, drawing cyclones off the Bay of Bengal.

Cyclones are severe storms that form over tropical oceans. They have extremely high winds and heavy rain. The east coast of India is at risk from cyclones, especially the low-lying Ganges Delta.

The monsoon and cyclones are both hazards in the region. For example, in 1990 a cyclone in April killed 140,000 people in Bangladesh and affected the lives of 12 million people. The damage was estimated at $1.8 million. In May about 1,000 people were killed when a cyclone hit Andhra Pradesh in southeast India. It affected nearly 9 million people and caused $600 million in damage. Then in July, severe flooding killed hundreds of people in northern and central India, with more deaths in Bangladesh when the Brahmaputra overflowed its banks.

The Ganges River Basin

▶ **The Ganges River affects India's landscape and people.**

The Ganges River Basin

The Ganges is one of the world's longest rivers, flowing more than 1,560 miles from its source in the Himalayas to its delta in the Bay of Bengal. This huge river valley cuts India in two. The river deposits rich **alluvial** silt on its flood plain, creating fertile farming land. This supports a region of high population density running from northwest to southeast along the Ganges Valley. For instance, in the Indian state of West Bengal, population density reaches 1,960 people per sq. mi.

The Ganges begins high in the Himalayas where it is created by melting snow and ice. At this point it is a fast-flowing stream full of white, turbulent water flowing through steep, narrow valleys and eroding material from the valley floor and sides. By the time it reaches its mouth, the Ganges' channel is more than 5 miles wide, meandering across a large valley. The sediment deposited by the river forms silt islands, which form a delta.

This view shows how India's farm land is densely cultivated right up to the edges of the river banks.

Crowds and an elephant bathe in the waters of the Ganges River in Varanasi.

The river and religion

The majority of India's population is Hindu, and for them the Ganges River is a sacred and holy place. According to ancient Hindu legend, the river once flowed through heaven. For devotees of Hinduism, the most famous place to visit on the river is Varanasi (Benares). One million people a year make a pilgrimage to this place to bathe and cleanse themselves from sin. They throw flowers, money, and food into the waters as a sacrifice. Another tradition is that Hindus scatter the ashes of their dead relatives there. The river is an important place in the daily worship and activities of the people and in the customs and traditions surrounding death.

Introducing India

This map shows the course of the Ganges River from its source to its mouth.

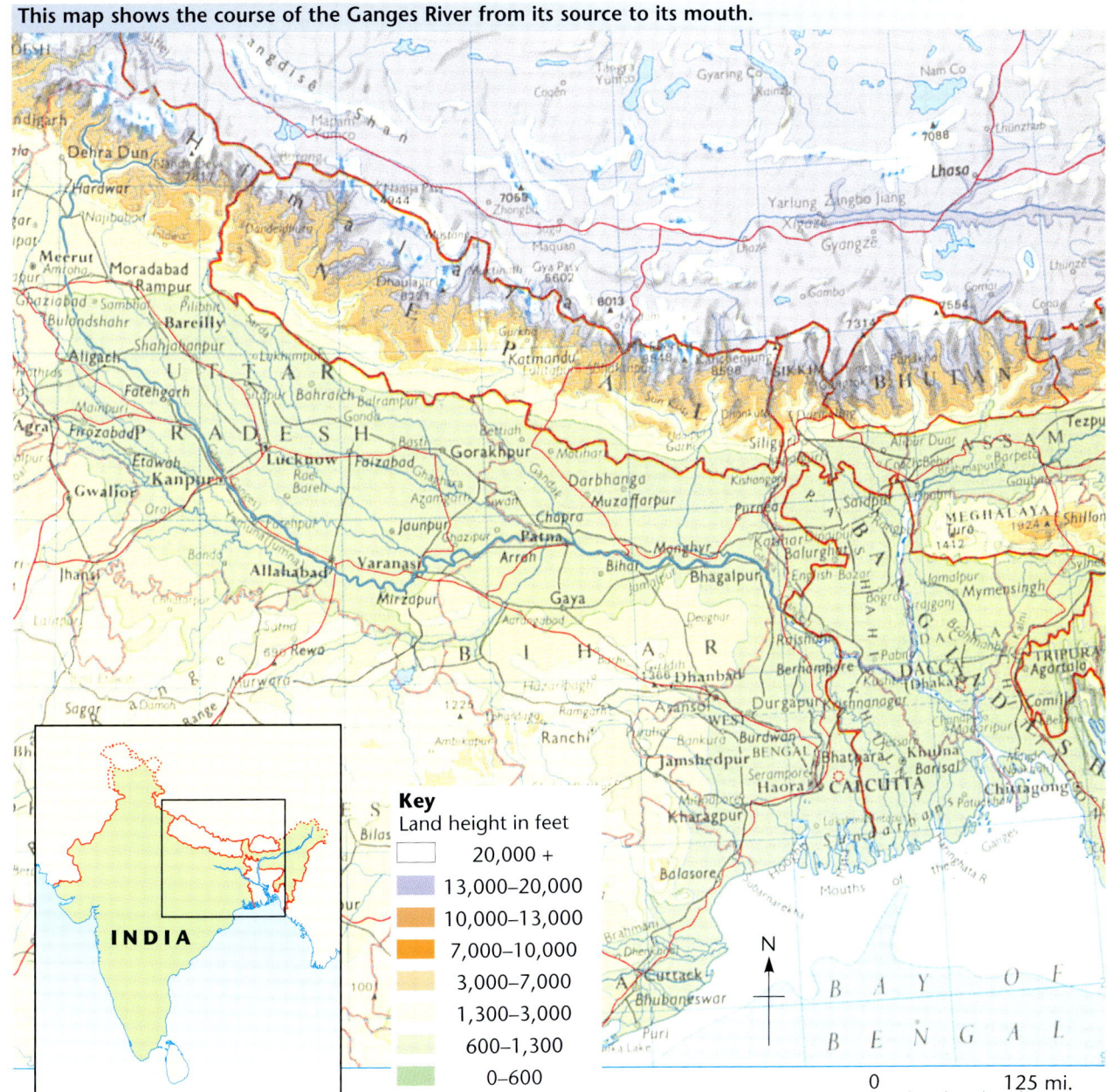

FACT FILE

The Ganges River

Length: 1,560 miles (36th longest in the world and 16th longest in Asia)
Drainage basin: 378,000 sq. mi. (5th largest in the world)

The Ganges River carries millions of tons of silt, eroded from the slopes of the Himalayas. For part of the year when flood water recedes, more than a half million acres of land become available for cultivation. However, pressure from farming and deforestation over the last century has worsened soil erosion and increased the flood hazard in the Ganges flood plain and its delta.

The Ganges waters are vital to the people living alongside the river. The Ganges is also the home of many endangered species, such as crocodiles. But the river is heavily polluted, partly from the ashes of 40,000 people cremated every year at Varanasi, but mainly from industry along its banks, especially in the city of Kanpur.

INVESTIGATION

Earthquakes

▶ Earthquakes have an impact on India.
▶ People try to return to normal lives after an earthquake disaster.

The Latur earthquake

On the evening of September 30, 1993, the Latur region of East Maharashtra, central India, was hit by an **earthquake** measuring 6.4 on the **Richter Scale**. The earthquake completely destroyed more than 100 villages, leaving 150,000 people homeless and more than 9,000 dead. Many organizations came to the aid of earthquake victims, including charities and the Indian army and government.

> "Killari village was at the center. We rushed there, it was beyond imagination. The whole village was destroyed and there were bodies everywhere. We tried to remove the bodies and help people trapped in the debris. Our main aim in the first fifteen days was to give relief to the victims—medical care, food, clothing, and shelter."

Dr. Lohiya, from Manavlok, an Indian development charity, describes the earthquake.

Responses to the earthquake

After the earthquake, people began to plan for the future. A local farmer said, "It was a difficult time, we had nothing. The sowing season had started, and we had no seed to plant."

Paveen Mahajan described the response of Janarth, an Indian development organization. "We needed to bring people back to normal life. As 90 percent of the workforce is involved in agriculture, we decided to help farmers. Villagers who didn't own land were given loans to help start small enterprises. We also gave fertilizers to richer farmers on condition that the amount was repaid after the harvest."

The Indian government built temporary buildings, meaning to replace them with permanent homes. But a year after the earthquake, many people were still living in

The Latur earthquake caused widespread destruction to people's homes and property.

Introducing India

Location Map of Latur

Collision Margin

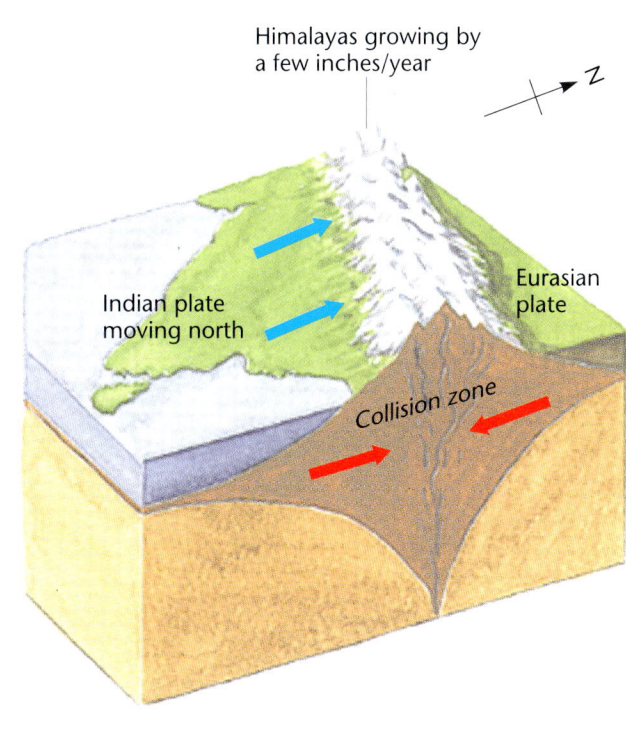

the temporary, concrete-roofed metal buildings. One man said, "Our old houses were large and clean. Now we have to live in tiny sheds!" Many people were also worried about how dangerous the new buildings would be if another earthquake struck.

Why do earthquakes occur in India?

Northern India is an unstable part of the earth's **crust**. It is close to the boundary between two **plates**. The Indian plate is moving about 2 inches north each year toward the Eurasian plate. Where the two plates meet is called a **collision plate margin**.

The collision of the two plates has two results. First, huge pressures build up until the crust moves suddenly and violently, causing an earthquake. Second, over millions of years, the pressure has forced the land upward into **fold mountains**. These are the Himalayas, the world's greatest **mountain chain**.

FACT FILE

Earthquakes

The strength of earthquakes is measured on the Richter Scale. This scale ranges from 1 or 2 (which can usually only be measured by special instruments) up to 9 (where the ground can be seen to shake and large fissures or gaps open up in the earth's surface). Each measurement on this scale marks an increase of a factor of 10. So an earthquake that reaches 8 on the Richter Scale is 10 times stronger than an earthquake that reaches 7.

In the year before the earthquake in Latur, 100 tremors were felt in this region. Tremors are often a sign that an earthquake may occur in the future. The Latur earthquake reached 6.4 on the Richter Scale. However the damage was much greater than that caused by much stronger earthquakes because the traditional houses in this area were built from stone. The houses had little resistance and many collapsed causing widespread damage and injuries.

15

2 POPULATION CHANGE AND URBANIZATION

Population Structure and Growth

▶ India has experienced a growth in population.

How does India count its population?

> With 900 million people India has the world's second biggest population after China. Every ten years India has a census to count its population. In 1991 "1,500,000 people knocked on every door, crossed inaccessible regions, entered slums, and stooped next to the thousands living on the streets to count India's population."
>
> *India Year Book*

Changes in population size

Populations change due to
- **birth rate**—number of children born.
- **death rate**—number of people who died.
- migration—people moving into or out of the country.

The difference between the birth and death rates is called the rate of **natural increase**.

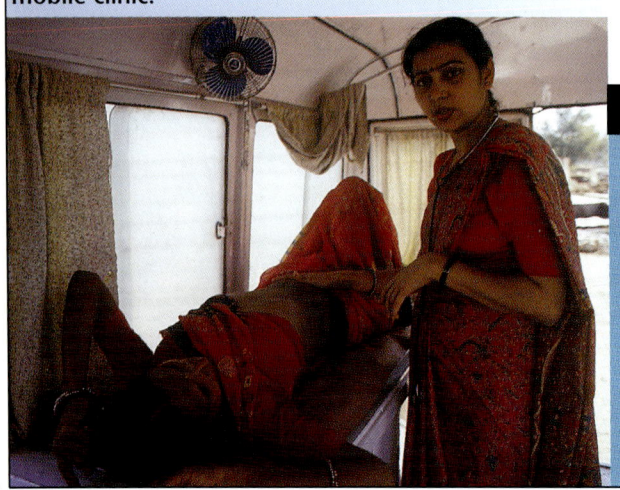

A doctor provides family planning advice from a mobile clinic.

India's population grew from 236 million in 1891 to 967 million people today, the result of a rapidly falling death rate and a birth rate that fell less sharply. Today the rate of population growth is about 2 percent.

Changes in India's Birth and Death Rates (per 1,000 people)

	1891	1901	1911	1921	1931	1941	1951	1961	1971	1981	1991
Births	48	46	49	48	47	44	41	42	41	36	30
Deaths	42	44	43	48	41	31	27	22	19	15	10

Birth rates and death rates can change for a number of reasons, including
- changes in health and sanitation.
- natural disasters.
- the availability of family planning.
- education for girls and women.
- changes in the age of marriage.
- changes in people's ideas about family size.
- changes in people's wealth and standard of living.

FAMILY PLANNING

During the 1970s India's government tried to reduce population growth by offering people incentives to become sterilized. But many people were forcibly sterilized, and this campaign ended in failure. Today India's family planning services are more widely available, and over 40 percent of Indian women choose to use the service. Better education for women and later marriages have also helped slow down population growth.

Population Change and Urbanization

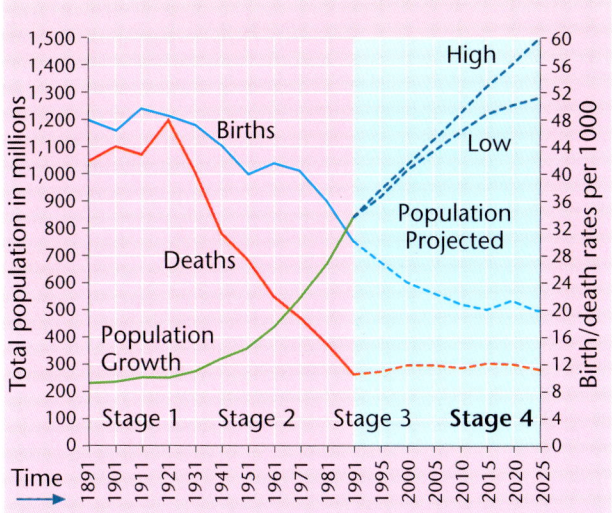

Population Growth Projections

THE DEMOGRAPHIC TRANSITION

A Demographic Transition Model

The graph to the left shows how population changes in a typical country. It helps explain how India's population may change in the future.

Stage 1   High Fluctuating Stage. Birth and death rates are both high, around 35/1,000. The population remains stable and low.

Stage 2   Early Expanding Stage. Birth rates remain high and death rates start to fall, reaching around 20/1,000. This leads to rapid population increase.

Stage 3   Late Expanding Stage. Birth rates fall rapidly, to around 20/1,000. Death rates continue to fall to around 15/1,000. Population still increases.

Stage 4   Low Fluctuating Stage. Birth and death rates are low and stable. Population growth slows down.

What is the impact of population growth?

Population growth creates extra demands for resources, jobs, and services. However, it is important to understand why people have larger families. In areas with few health services, parents may need to have five children in order to guarantee that three survive. Children's work can help support the family, and they provide security for their aging parents.

FACT FILE

India's children

India's population in mid-1996 was probably around 954 million. The most recent population census counted 844 million on March 1, 1991, of whom 438 million were male and 406 female. Population growth is now a little under 2 percent. The fertility rate in 1992 was four children per family, down from 6.2 children per family in 1965.

Life expectancy at birth increased from 32 years in 1951 to 61 years in 1992 and male life expectancy is now higher than in Russia. India's population is of such extreme diversity—of language, religion, caste, and class—that any simple categorization is very misleading.

The Economist, 1997

In India the role of children is very important. With few social services, many parents come to rely on the support of their own children in old age. The extended family, where different generations of the same family live together, is very common.

Within poorer communities children may also be a source of additional income for the family. It is estimated that of India's 206 million children, 17 million work. The majority of children work in agriculture and the construction industry. Many thousands work making carpets and also in matchstick factories. Here a nine-year-old girl, one of the 70,000 children who works in the matchstick factories of Tamil Nadu, describes her day.

"The factory bus picks me up at six in the morning to take me to work. In the factory I place the matches on a rack ready to be put in the boxes. I'm one of the fastest workers in the factory which means I get paid more. In the afternoon I pack the matches into boxes. This is a better job because it's not so cramped and my back and neck don't get as sore. By six o'clock the day's almost over, and I'll get my pay of eight rupees (12 cents). I'll spend one rupee on the bus to get home, leaving me seven rupees for the whole day. I've been working in the factory a long time—ever since I was a child.

Population and Development

▶ Population structure can be shown in a pyramid model.
▶ Population and development are linked.

Population structure

Population pyramids can be used to show the balance between men and women and the balance between different age groups. India's population pyramid for 1990 has a wide base, because there is a high proportion of young people. It also has steep sides, because life expectancy is fairly short. The large numbers of children in the graph below show that the birth rate is high and the population is growing. As the wide band of children become older, they are likely to have children of their own. This is known as a bottom heavy population pyramid. This pattern is common in economically developing countries.

The pyramid for the United States has more people in the middle range of ages 30 to 55 because of a phenomena called the postwar baby boom that followed World War II. This was when many people had children in a relatively short amount of time.

Population and development

The structure of a country's population has an important influence on a country's opportunities for development. The diversity of India's population presents many challenges, for example
- high rates of illiteracy.
- low status of women.
- demands on India's health service.
- demands for better employment opportunities, for example India has 3.6 million unemployed university graduates.

DEPENDENCY RATIO

A country's dependency ratio shows the number of people between the ages of 15 and 64 who are **economically active**, compared to people under 15 and over 64. However, this figure does not take into account the people who are unemployed or children who may be working.

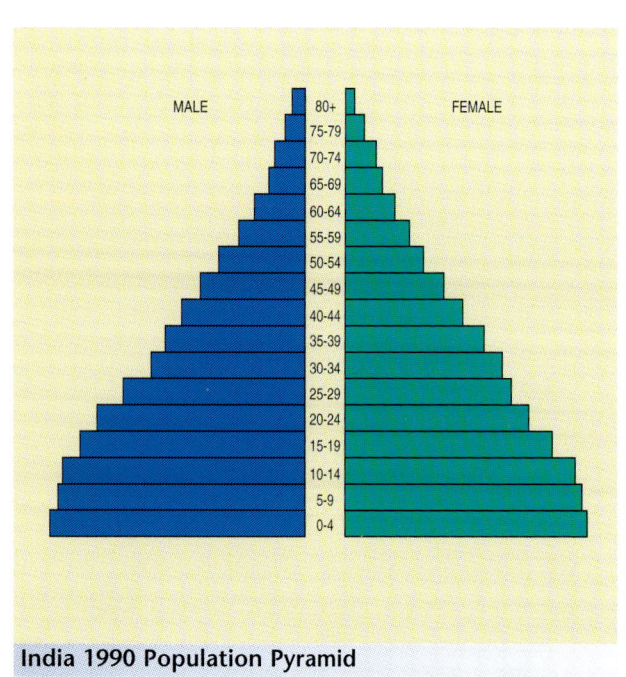

India 1990 Population Pyramid

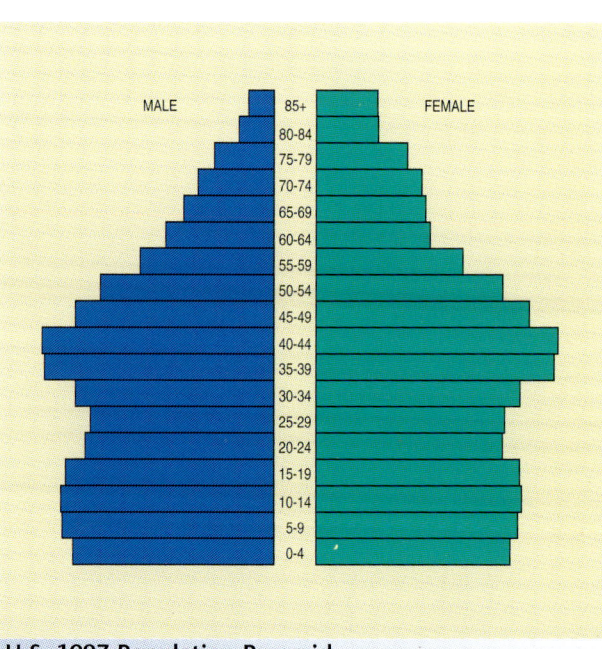

U.S. 1997 Population Pyramid

Population Change and Urbanization

India's dependency ratio 1990

$$\frac{\text{Economically inactive (children and people over 64)}}{\text{Economically active (workers)}} \times 100 = \frac{342{,}824{,}000}{503{,}381{,}000} \times 100 = 68\%$$

POPULATION DENSITY

The map shows the distribution of India's population. It shows population density, the average number of people per square mile.

India's Population Density (people per square mile)

	Male	Female
0–9	7.5	7
10–19	8.5	8
20–29	8.5	8
30–39	8	7.5
40–49	7	6.5
50–59	5.5	5
60–69	4	3.5
70+	2.5	3

India's Projected Population Structure in 2025

FACT FILE

Medicine

There are many highly-trained doctors in India, but traditional methods of medicine are still often used. After independence there was a renewal of old methods. The Indian traditional system of medicine is known as *Ayuveda* from *ayus* meaning "life" and *veda* meaning "knowledge." This method tries to cure disease by studying both mind and body. Most of the medicines are based on herbs, vegetables, or animal products. The Hindu god Shiva was the first herbalist and is sometimes shown as carrying herbs in one hand and a lotus flower in the other.

Yoga

Just as Indian medicine looks at both mind and body when curing disease, the philosophy of Yoga in India works at combining the body, mind, and spirit for maintaining health.

Yoga demands a long course of training. This includes
Yama, which is restraining aggressive and undisciplined behavior; it insists on no stealing, no lies, no violence, and no unnecessary possessions;
Niyama, which is restraining one's own body; no anger, no selfishness, and resigning oneself to what life brings, and
Asanas, which is learning certain exercises and postures, some of which are well-known in the West.

Yoga also includes training to learn how to control one's breathing and senses and how to meditate or control one's thoughts. Yogis, or people who have practiced yoga for many years, are capable of extraordinary feats, such as stopping and starting their own heartbeat.

Urbanization and Migration

▶ India's people move to the urban areas.

Urbanization
India's countryside is home to 74 percent of the population, but towns and cities are growing at a rate of 3 percent a year.

Urban growth is caused by
- **n**atural increase, when there are more births than deaths in the city.
- **r**ural-urban migration, when people move into towns from the countryside.

Why do people migrate?
Cities often offer the prospect of a better quality of life than rural areas. For example, in the city of Bangalore more than 52 percent of male **migrants** said better employment was their reason for moving. Social reasons also contribute to migration, particularly for women, with 75 percent of Bangalore's female migrants saying they moved because of family responsibilities.

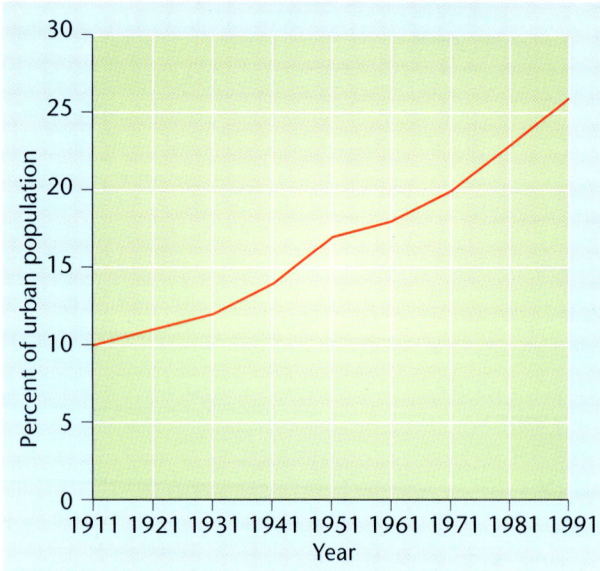

Growth in Percent of Urban Population

The city of Ahmedabad has shanty settlements in areas of unused land.

Where do the migrants live?
While many migrants move to good accommodations, others end up living in shanty towns and temporary housing. Here migrants often build the houses themselves out of wood and other materials, usually on unused land such as alongside railroad lines or roadsides. Because these areas are unplanned, they are often known as **informal settlements**. They usually lack services, such as running water or trash collection, and have little chance of getting services. Although these settlements look dilapidated, they contain a range of **small-scale** industries and services.

Quality of Life: Urban-Rural Contrasts

	Urban	Rural
Access to proper sanitation	50%	2.5%
% living in poverty	20%	33%
Infant Mortality Rate (IMR)	50/1,000	86/1,000
Total household assets (in Rupees)	Ru 41,000	Ru 36,000
% living within 1/2 mi. of doctor	47%	20%

Population Change and Urbanization

Reasons for Migration

Lokech: "Farming's hard work. If I don't get a good crop I'll sell out and leave."

Geeta: "My cousin lives in Bangalore. He said there are good jobs and decent schools for my children."

Binu: "In my village my caste is looked down on. In a city I could live my own life."

Urmilla: "The doctor's an hour's bus journey away. The health services here are poor."

Maya: "I'm moving to marry. My future husband lives in Madras."

Dhiraj: "I'd earn more money in the city."

Problems of informal settlements are
- lack of sanitation, water, and electricity.
- high living densities, families living in single rooms.
- some cities try to clear informal settlements by bulldozing them. Many shanty towns are liable to flood or are built next to trash dumps.

Informal settlements provide
- cheap accommodation that people can build themselves.
- employment opportunities.
- a first foothold in the city.

Other migrations in India

Migration has not only occurred from rural to urban areas. One of the largest migrations in India was at Independence in 1947 when the country was divided into India and Pakistan. During this period 15 million people migrated between these two countries. Many Indians have also migrated further to Europe, North America, Eastern Africa, the Caribbean, and the Middle East. Money sent back to India from these migrants brings $5 billion into the Indian economy.

FACT FILE

Differences between rural and urban India

	Rural	Urban
Average age of marriage for girls	16.5 years old	17.5 years old
Population growth rate 1981–91	3.1%	1.8%
Number of households	94 million	29 million
Birth rate/1,000 (1990)	32	25
Death rate/1,000 (1990)	11	7
Use of electricity for lighting	15%	64%

Life in India's Cities

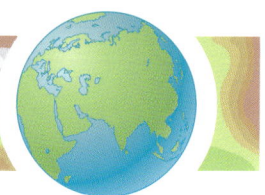

▶ **Problems come with urban life.**

Delhi bans Smokers as Pollution Solution
"Delhi has banned public smoking to clean up its foul air. Delhi is the world's most polluted city, with 7,500 people dying from respiratory illnesses caused by vehicle emission and industrial smog."

The Sunday Telegraph

India's urban areas

India's cities provide many scenes which would not seem out of place in a city from an economically developed country, such as high-rise apartments, industrial developments, stores, traffic-filled roads, and busy offices. However, alongside these are also the shanty developments and informal economy that are a feature of high rural-urban migration.

One problem of urban development is air pollution caused by the growth of traffic and industry. It is estimated that 40,000 deaths per year are related to India's pollution. This has led to some drastic steps being taken.

Industries have also been responsible for accidents such as the Bhopal disaster in 1984, when a cloud of poisonous gas escaped from the Union Carbide chemical factory in Bhopal. Most of the 15,000 victims lived in areas of poor housing situated around the edge of the factory. In 1997 claims for compensation from the American owners still continued.

Urban areas are the main locations for India's industrial development because they need facilities, such as power and good communications, as well as employees. This has helped create an **urban bias**, with a wide divide growing up between rural and urban areas. For example, urban wage rates are three times those in rural areas.

The Hiranandani complex is just one of Mumbai's (Bombay's) growing number of expensive housing developments.

Tenement housing provides accommodations for much of Mumbai's (Bombay's) population.

22

Population Change and Urbanization

Urbanization has led to the expansion of cities into rural areas through **peri-urban growth**. This is where new settlements develop on the edges of cities. The peri-urban growth settlement of Anand Gram, shown in the map below, is located 9 miles from central Delhi. The settlement was started on an uninhabited part of a flood plain. Today 200 people live there. People work both in farming and in urban jobs. The community has improved the area by providing a well for water, electricity, sanitation, brick buildings, a job training center, and a recreational field for playing the game of cricket.

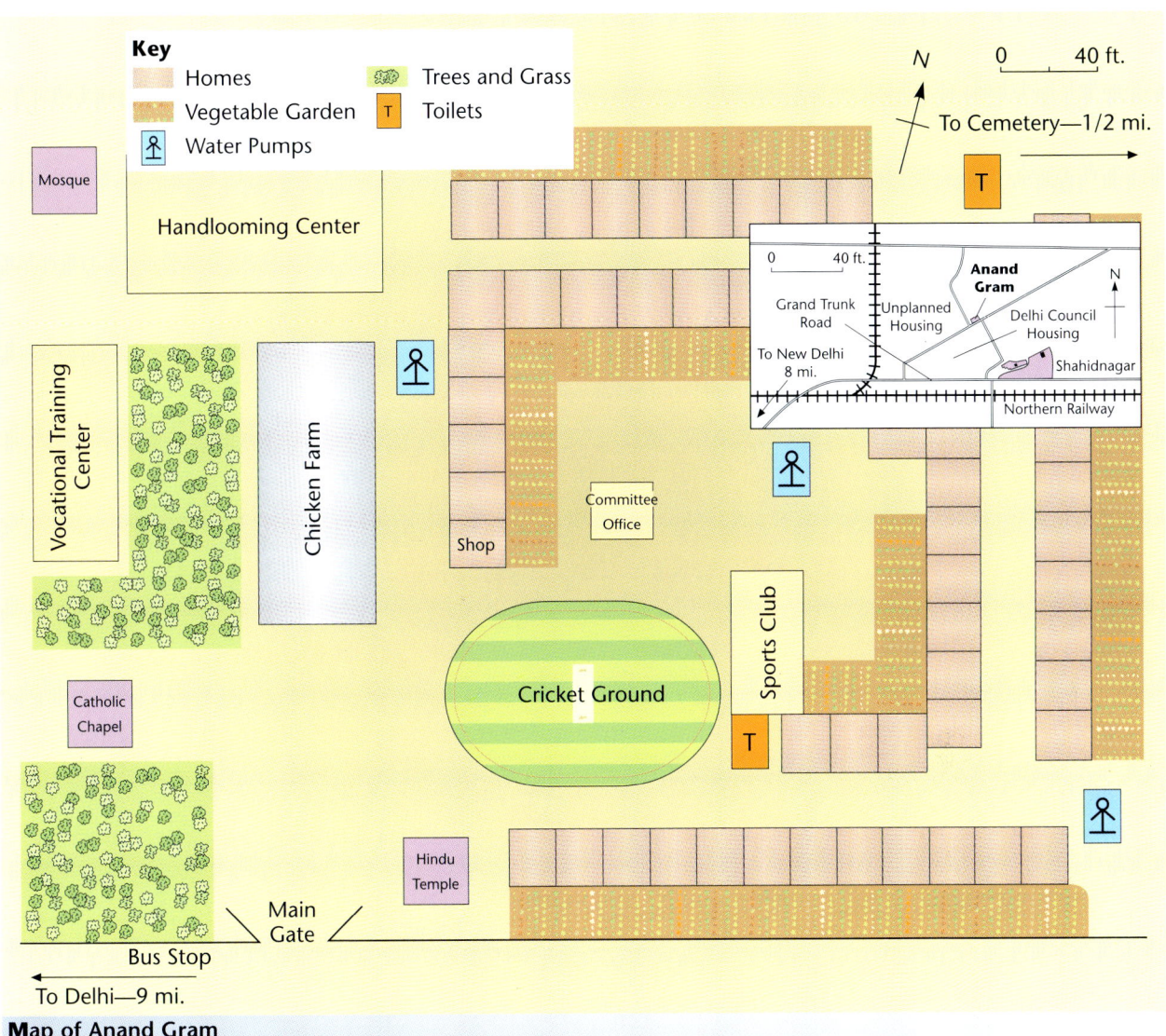

Map of Anand Gram

FACT FILE

Shanty towns

Bombay is now called Mumbai.

"High-rise or Hovel—It's All Hot Property"

For sale: One-room shanty in Bombay's Mahim Creek area. No electricity, no running water, no view—except of children splashing in an open sewer. Price $6,700. Whether you are searching for a hovel or for a high-rise, Bombay has become the third most expensive city in the world. Bombay probably has more millionaires than London, but many middle-class Indians—a teacher earning $90 a month—cannot afford the expensive rents. Many are forced to move to satellite suburbs a two-hour train ride away. Bombay's port, which handles half of India's foreign trade, and its factories, generating more than 30 percent of Gross Domestic Product, exerts a strong pull on Indians in the countryside who are desperate for work.

The Independent, March 19, 1995

INVESTIGATION

Bangalore

▶ Life has variety in Bangalore.

Diversity in Bangalore

Bangalore with its nearly five million inhabitants is the capital city of Karnataka state. It was founded in 1537 on high ground 3,280 feet above sea level. This was a good defensive position to control the trade routes between Mysore and Madras. Bangalore became an important fortress, particularly during the 1800s when Tipu Sultan defended this area against the British colonists. After the defeat of Tipu Sultan, the British expanded the city. Its altitude provided a cooler climate that was more bearable for the colonists.

Modern Bangalore is a clean, spacious, and well-planned city. It was once known as the Garden City of India, but it's name in the language of Karnataka state means "town of boiled beans."

Bangalore is rapidly advancing toward becoming a "City of the Future." It is now India's fifth largest city.

Year	Number of People
1941	411,000
1951	786,000
1961	1,203,000
1971	1,664,000
1981	2,922,000
1991	4,087,000
1996 (est.)	5,000,000

Population Growth in Bangalore

Life styles in Bangalore

As with all Indian cities, there is a wide range of lifestyles in Bangalore. It is one of India's boom towns due to the growth of electronics factories which have created much wealth.

> "It is said that Bangalore is the fastest growing city in Asia, and definitely India's yuppie heaven."
>
> *Lonely Planet Guide*

However, this wealth exists alongside poverty. The city's rapid growth has also produced many problems. These include

- high level of unemployment. Low paid, informal jobs like collecting waste paper for recycling pays 20 Rupees (30 cents) a day.
- a shortage of adequate housing—more than 500,000 people live in very poor housing.
- stress on city services, such as water supply and sanitation. In 1941 the water supply per person per day was 26 gallons. This fell to 12 gallons in 1988.
- severe traffic congestion.

This shanty building in Bangalore will be replaced with luxury penthouses and apartments.

Population Change and Urbanization

Land use in Bangalore

The city center has developed as two areas around the historic hill fort and British soldiers' quarters. Today central Bangalore forms a crescent area of businesses, shops, and offices. This area, known as the **central business district (CBD)**, is shown in the land-use map below. To the west, south, and southeast, the CBD is circled by a wide area of lower-cost housing. This pattern is broken in the north and northeast where a sector of high-cost housing reaches the outskirts. To the northwest, factories developed on an area of flat land alongside major roads and rail links. Areas of poor buildings are scattered across the city, although they are mainly located at the outskirts or alongside main roads and railroads where people can occupy the land.

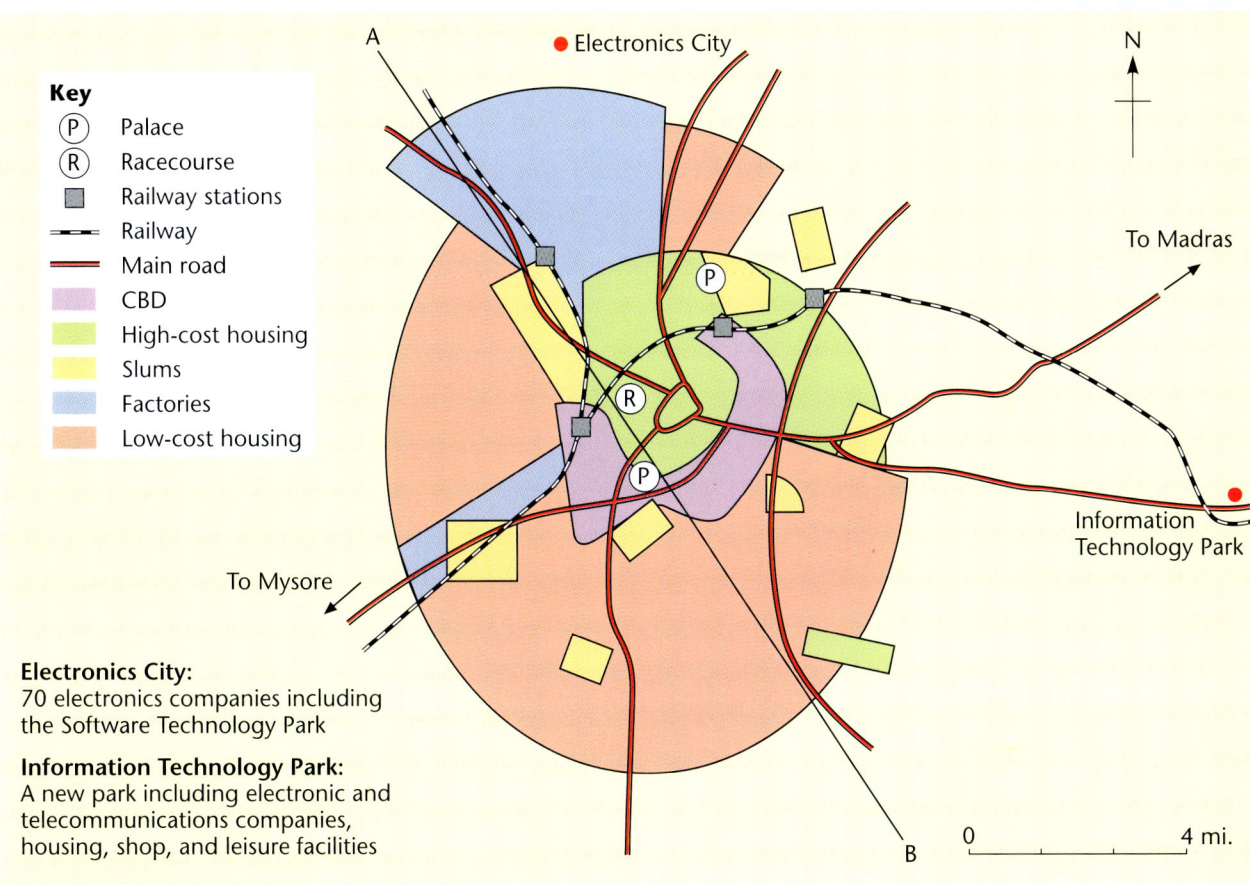

Electronics City: 70 electronics companies including the Software Technology Park

Information Technology Park: A new park including electronic and telecommunications companies, housing, shop, and leisure facilities

Land-Use Map

FACT FILE

Industrial planning in Bangalore
Karnataka state's industrial policy has helped economic growth in Bangalore. The city has eleven industrial areas between 9 and 25 miles from the city, with more planned. The state buys and develops the land, putting in services such as water, power and telephone links, and industrial units.

Electronics City was established in 1978. It is the largest concentration of electronics companies in Bangalore, including Motorola (communications equipment) and Hewlett Packard (computers). Nearby, Electronics City 2 is opening up.

Information Technology Park was begun in 1995 and is due to be completed in 1999, costing $300 million to build. Nearby is an **Exports Promotion Park**. It is close to the airport and inland container terminal. It will contain non-polluting industries, such as electronics, software, clothing, and machine tools.

Bangalore's plan to build industrial parks outside the city has some disadvantages. Many employees have to commute by bus from the city over poor roads. There are also problems with water and electricity supply. Also, over time, these industrial parks may speed up the outward spread of the city.

3 RURAL DEVELOPMENT

Rural India

▶ Small and large farms are found in India.

New agricultural machinery is being used to plow fields in Gujarat.

India's rural areas
India is sometimes described as a nation of 800,000 villages. Over 60 percent of India's people work in the rural areas. Examples of people's work include the shepards of the Himalayan foothills and the wheat farmers of the Punjab. The country also includes the paddy fields of Bengal and the tea plantations of the Nilgiri Hills. Although most people in the country work in agriculture, there are also other activities such as forestry, mining, small-scale manufacturing, and services.

The monsoon
Because only 30 percent of India's farms are irrigated, rural life is closely connected to the **monsoon's** rainfall pattern. The monsoon produces three farming seasons during the year—the hot season, the monsoon season, and the cool season.

Farmers in states such as Karnataka, Maharashtra, Orissa, Tamil Nadu, and Madhya Pradesh rely greatly on the monsoon rains. A 1 percent drop in rainfall can lead to a 0.5 percent drop in harvests. In the Punjab, Haryana, Kerala, Assam, and Andrha Pradesh, irrigation and scientific farming means that farmers no longer depend totally on the monsoon.

Farming types
Many of India's farms are small scale and run by families. These farms often grow food crops, such as rice, wheat, and vegetables to be eaten by the family themselves. Extra crops are also grown that are sold to earn money. These farms are often only a few acres in size, use small amounts of **pesticides** and **fertilizers**, and do not use much technology.

Commercial farms grow cash crops, including sugar, tea, coffee, spices, cotton, rice, and wheat. Commercial farms are often large and employ laborers to work the land. These farms also use mechanization, pesticides, and fertilizers. Investing in these technologies is expensive, so family farms are often less likely to grow cash crops. Jobs on commercial farms provide employment for the 30 percent of Indian rural families who do not have enough land to support themselves.

	1980	1995
Sugar	129	285
Cotton	7.0	9.4
Rice	53.6	80
Wheat	36.3	65.2

(millions tons EIU reference)

Agricultural Production [*The Economist*]

Rural Development

PLANTATIONS

The British forced Indians to grow cash crops such as cotton, jute, indigo, coffee, tea, and sugar, for export back to Britain. Tea was first sold in Britain in the 17th century. Tea and the other crops were often grown in large British-owned estates called **plantations**. Plantations covered many thousands of acres and often reduced the land available for food crops. The importance of these crops continues today. Tea production is almost 1.8 billion pounds.

Farmers transplant rice in paddy fields in Kashmir.

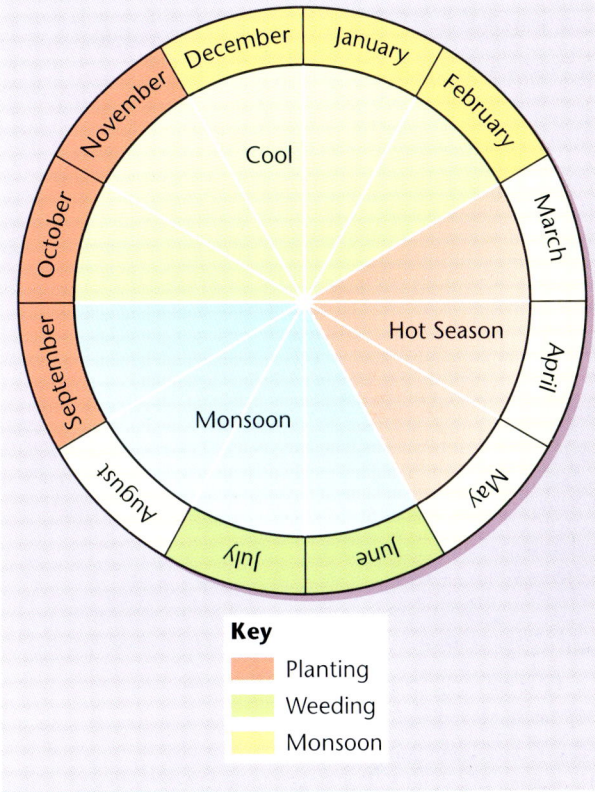

This agricultural calendar shows the farming cycle.

FACT FILE

Diet

Many Indian meals begin with a selection of chutneys and vegetables with spicy sauces. It is usually served with poppadoms (very thin, fried disks made of lentil flour). Meat, chicken, or vegetables are served with rice as a main course. They are often eaten with chapattis, a type of thin, bread pancake used to scoop up the food. Spices such as chili, cumin, cinnamon, coriander, and ginger are used in many Indian dishes. The meal is often finished off with fresh fruit or a sweet dish. Kulfi, a type of ice cream, is popular in hot weather. In rural India people usually sit on the floor or on small wooden stools to eat. The food is often served on a sheet or tablecloth on the floor.

Food varies from region to region. In northern India, the curries tend to be quite hot. People also eat dried beans and lentils (dal), Tandoori food (meat, chicken, and puffy naan bread cooked in a dome-shaped charcoal oven called a tandoor), and Basmati rice grown on the northern plains.

Near the western coast fish is served, and the food is milder. The hottest curry of all, Madras curry, comes from the south. Bengal in the east is famous for its sweets, such as the pretzel-shaped jelabis, which are first deep-fried and then dipped in sweet red syrup.

The Green Revolution

▶ Agriculture is changing in India.

The beginning of the Green Revolution

In the 1950s India could not grow enough food for its population and often had to rely on food aid, especially from the United States. But a series of agricultural changes, known as the **Green Revolution**, changed this situation. Scientists set out to improve farming by increasing crop yields, particularly for cash crops. The changes included
- introducing **high yielding varieties** (HYVs) of crops, particularly wheat and rice, to give better harvests.
- using chemical **fertilizers** and **pesticides**.
- increasing irrigation.
- increasing mechanization.
- making farms bigger.

These changes have been very important for India. By 1990, India moved from food shortages to producing a food surplus, especially in rice and wheat.

India to be Third Biggest Rice Exporter
"India, which struggled to achieve self-sufficiency, will become the world's third largest rice exporter (the U.S. and Thailand). Aided by eight good monsoons and easier exports, India exported 900,000 tons of rice in 1994–1995."

Financial Times

The Green Revolution in the Punjab

Conditions in the Punjab were ideal for the Green Revolution. The Punjab is located in northwest India, an area with many rivers and irrigation canals. Over 80 percent of its land is suitable for agriculture, compared to the Indian average of 50 percent. Much of the land is also irrigated. Farming in the Punjab is so successful that although it only makes up 1.5 percent of India's land area, the Punjab accounts for 11 percent of India's agricultural production.

The patchwork landscape is fields and irrigation channels in an intensively farmed area of Ladakh.

In the Punjab, the Green Revolution has lead to mechanized farming, including the use of combine harvesters.

Rural Development

The Green Revolution at the Village Level

	1955	1965	1978	1986
% of crops land irrigated	60%	80%	100%	100%
Mechanization	none	none	four tractors	nine tractors
Population	876	–	–	1076
Average size of farms	4.8 acres	–	5.7 acres	–
Weed control	Hoeing and plowing used to control weeds			Herbicides used to control weeds
Wage labor rates		300% increase in incomes from 1965–78		
Land prices		5-fold increase from 1965–78		
Cropping as % of cropped area				
Summer crops				
corn	21%	–	–	40%
rice	0%	–	–	10%
winter crops				
wheat	21%	–	–	69%
fodder	10%	–	–	1%
chick peas	6%	–	–	1%
Fertilizer		Increase by 300% between 1955 and 1986		
Increase in crop yields				
Wheat (tons/acre)	.5%	–	–	1%
Rice (tons/acre)	.4%	–	–	1%

Problems of the Green Revolution

Despite the increased harvests, there have been problems created by the Green Revolution. Because new seeds, fertilizers, and technology cost money, many poorer farmers have not gained from these changes. As farms became bigger, more small farmers became landless and unable to grow food for their families. Instead the small farmers often work for larger farmers. The use of pesticides has polluted some water supplies, and the increasing use of water for irrigation lowered the **water table** in many places making it more difficult to get water from underground.

Increased harvests were based on the introduction of high yielding variety (HYV) seeds. These required careful attention, including the use of pesticides and artificial fertilizers.

FACT FILE
The effects of the Green Revolution

Population growth, food production, and consumption in India, 1980-95			
Year	1980	1990	1995
Population (millions)	689	827	931
Food consumption (kcals/person/day)	1,959	2,297	2,395
Food production (per person 1980 = 100)	100	116	120

Agricultural Development in the Thar Desert

▶ **The desert has turned green.**

"I have a dream of seeing these great deserts where hardly anything grows converted into fertile lands."

Kanwar Sain, chief engineer of the Indira Gandhi Canal

Geographical background
The Thar Desert is a harsh environment. It receives less than 12 inches of rainfall a year and has poor soils. Poor health, poor education, high infant mortality, and female literacy as low as 2 percent make life difficult for local people.

Traditional farming
Traditional farmers in the Thar Desert keep herds of sheep, cattle, goats, and camels. They graze over large areas, often with long **migrations**, to find pasture. Everyone shares grazing rights to **common land** that no one owns. Only small areas have enough water to grow drought resistant crops, such as **sorghum**.

Change in the Thar Desert
Building the Indira Gandhi Canal began in 1957. The project has already brought water to 1.2 million acres at a cost of over $1 billion. It has brought big changes to local farmers, including
- more irrigated land.
- wealthier farmers irrigating their land for crops, rather than grazing animals.
- more cash crops such as chilies and mustard.
- more jobs in fields alongside the canal.
- three times more mechanization (for example, tractors) than before the project.

These changes have also led to problems.
- Some farmers have taken over common land, replacing grazing land with private fields.
- The soil in many areas has lost its fertility through salination. When irrigation water dries, salt is left behind.
- Many local soils have **eroded** because they are unsuitable for crops.
- Cash crops require more water, so water supplies are reduced. For example, chilies need sixteen times more water than sorghum.
- Hollows in the desert have become waterlogged. Some people now fish in the middle of the desert.
- Many poorer farmers cannot take advantage of the new changes.

Shepards in Rajasthan herd sheep, cattle, goats, and camels over large distances to find water and pastures.

Rural Development

DEVELOPMENT IN THE THAR DESERT

The URMUL Trust, an Indian nongovernment organization (NGO), works with 60,000 people in the Thar Desert. It identified four reasons for poverty.

- Indebtedness
- Poor health
- Increase of private fields instead of common land
- Wealthier farmers claiming water and land rights from poorer people

URMUL tried to overcome these problems by

- providing loans.
- supporting village health workers.
- protecting areas of common land.
- supporting the community's fight for better water and land rights.

The canal has accounted for much of the northwest state of Rajasthan's agricultural expenditure, leaving few resources for other small-scale investments in farming.

The water from the major canals of the Indira Gandhi Canal plan is distributed to smaller canals where electric pumps can irrigate the farmer's fields.

Location Map of the Thar Desert

FACT FILE

The Thar Desert

There is a plan to extend the Indira Gandhi Canal, but the nongovernment organization, URMUL, believes that priority must be given to the poor if they are to benefit at all.

"The Indira Gandhi Canal Project must be one of the greatest human engineering achievements. However, we must ask ourselves what can be done to make the project more meaningful to the largest number of people? All the issues URMUL raises address the immediate problems of waterlogging and settlement. In a sense these are only symptoms—the real problem is in the lack of a people's voice in planning and decision making. Poorer farmers are drawn into a vicious cycle of mounting debts as they struggle to develop less favorable plots of land. It is so important to give priority to the poor because with the loss of land, they suffer more than the loss of a resource or money; it is part of the social fabric of existence."

URMUL Trust Report on Indira Gandhi Canal

31

Small-Scale Farming in the Nilgiri Hills

▶ **Many farmers rely on small-scale farming.**

Farmers in Karnataka state carry the rice harvest back to their village.

Family farms

The Nilgiri Hills is one area where many people rely on **small-scale** farming for their livelihood. Most farmers in this area have very small plots of land, often less than 3.7 acres in size. On this they grow a wide range of **food crops** such as rice, bananas, potatoes, onions, and vegetables.

These crops are mainly grown to be eaten by the farmers' families, but some crops will be sold for extra cash. Animals are an expensive investment and most of the farmers can afford to keep only a few chickens, and possibly a pig or a cow. Almost all **farm labor** is provided by the family, although people also work for wealthier farmers who mainly grow cash crops.

Cash crops

Cash crops, such as tea, coffee, and ginger, are often grown by farmers who can afford to buy **pesticides**, seed, and **fertilizer**. It is often difficult for small farmers to grow cash crops because they cannot afford the cost or cannot risk a crop failure.

Here is a breakdown for ginger production costs.
- Cost of renting a field: $6 a season, which is about one year.
- Cost of buying pesticides and hiring workers to plant and harvest the field: $190.
- Income from selling the crop of ginger: $1,270.

FAMILY FARMS

Input		Output	
Land:	small plots less than 3.7 acres, often owned by the family	**Crops:**	wide range of food crops grown, mainly for family consumption
Labor:	family	**Animals:**	milk, meat from small animals, eggs
Technology:	low levels, mainly hand tools or plowing with animals, little use of pesticides or fertilizers	**Labor:**	some family members may work on richer farmers' land
Crops:	wide range of different food crops grown from seeds	**Income:**	small income for family from sale of surplus food crops, some income from paid work
Animals:	provide manure for fertilizer, used to pull plows		

The farmers who own land or who can afford to rent larger fields can get a bigger harvest and a larger income.

They also have enough money to buy more farm animals, which they can raise to sell.

These farmers also provide jobs, such as hoeing and harvesting, for small-scale farmers, but pay is often little more than 60 cents a day and the work is only available eight months a year.

Excess food crops are often sold in local markets, such as this market in the village of Chembakolli in Tamil Nadu.

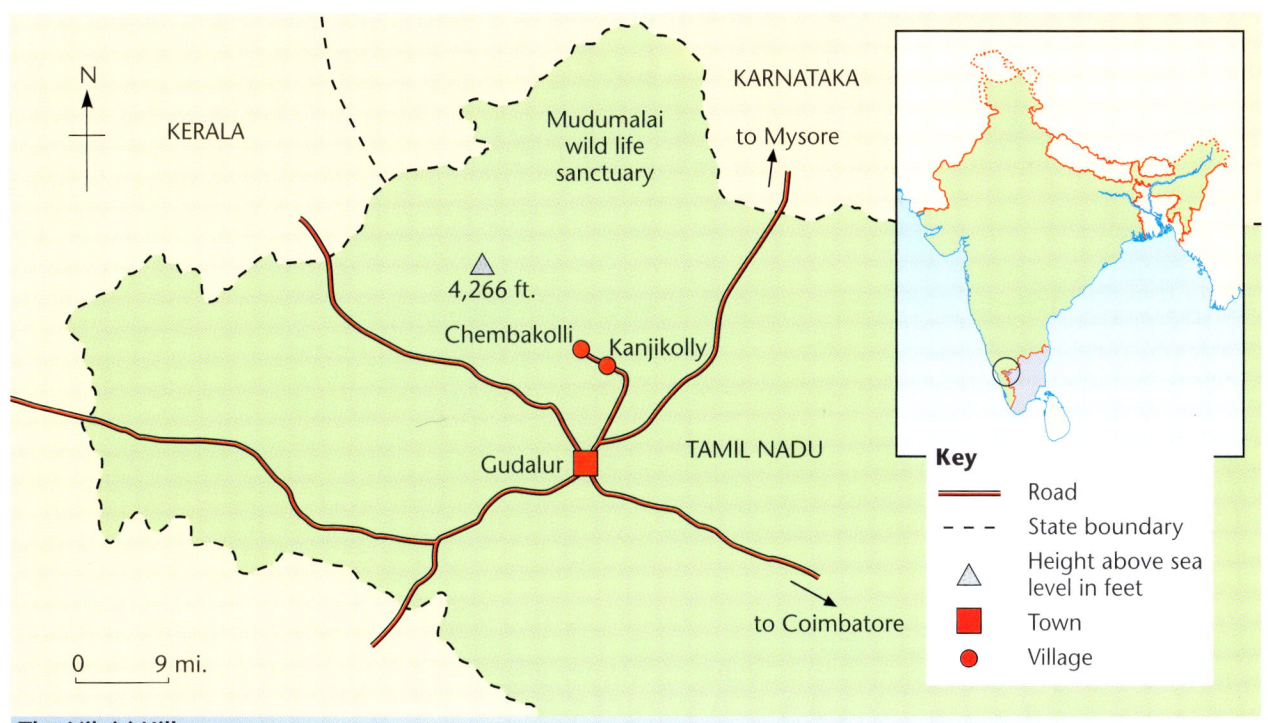

The Nilgiri Hills

FACT FILE

The Nilgiri Hills

The Nilgiri Hills (Blue Hills) stretch over an area of 980 square miles in the state of Tamil Nadu in the south of India. The region has an equatorial climate, and its natural vegetation is tropical rainforest. Of the 700,000 people who live in the Nilgiri Hills, 80 percent are small-scale farmers. Tea and coffee plantations take up more than 50 percent of the cultivated land.

The clearance of the land for plantations has not only affected the population of small-scale farmers in the Nilgiri Hills, it has also removed the forests that supported much of this area's wildlife. This area is home to wildlife, such as deer, monkeys, and a wide range of birds.

One other animal common to this area is the elephant. Elephants are kept by people to help with logging.

The Nilgiri Hills are quite high (7,575 feet). Hill stations were developed as refuges from the heat in British colonial times. Ootacamund, "the Queen of the Hill Stations" in the Nilgiri Hills, is a popular tourist destination. Ootacamund is the name given by the British to Udhagamandalam. It is popularly referred to as "Ooty."

INVESTIGATION

Tea Plantations

▶ The growth of cash crops has had an impact on India.

Tea—a cash crop

The hot, moist conditions in the Nilgiri Hills of southern India support a tropical rainforest ecosystem. The area has a wide variety of climates and vegetation that is special in India.

The Adivasi are a group of people who live in the Nilgiri Hills. Their name means "the original people of the forest." Because their ancestors lived here for many hundreds of years, they have rights to use the forest's land and resources. Adivasi families farm small plots of land, growing mainly **food crops**.

Many Adivasi families are poor, living on about 200 Rupees ($2.50) a week. They are also treated as inferiors by other people, especially those who want to farm Adivasi land for themselves.

Much of the forest has been developed for commercial agriculture, particularly tea and coffee **plantations**. In the Nilgiri Hills the plantations have brought some low-paid jobs into the area. As one worker said, "I pick tea with my mother. For picking 25 kilos [55 pounds] in a day, I get 25 Rupees [30 cents]." But plantations have also produced conflicts over the use of land.

The introduction of tea and coffee plantations resulted in a major change in the land use of the Nilgiri Hills.

PLANTATION AGRICULTURE

The plantations bring both positive and negative changes.

Positive:

- The crops are sold to consumers in India and overseas.
- Tea bushes have to be picked every fifteen days, providing tea-picking jobs.
- Workers are needed to transport, process, and pack the crops.

Negative:

- The plantations reduce the land available to the Adivasi.
- Tea picking is a poorly paid job.
- Workers often have poor job security and conditions.

The Adivasi people of the Nilgiri Hills demonstrate in support of their rights to land.

Rural Development

To overcome the problem of losing their land, the Adivasi, helped by a local charity, employed land-rights lawyers to represent them in court. Their land was mapped so no one else could claim it, and they held a peaceful demonstration of 30,000 people. This showed that they would not allow their land rights to be easily overturned. One Adivasi said, "Everyone was told about our land-rights and that we shouldn't fear people who threatened us. We all worked together, and now we've enough land and our spirit has returned."

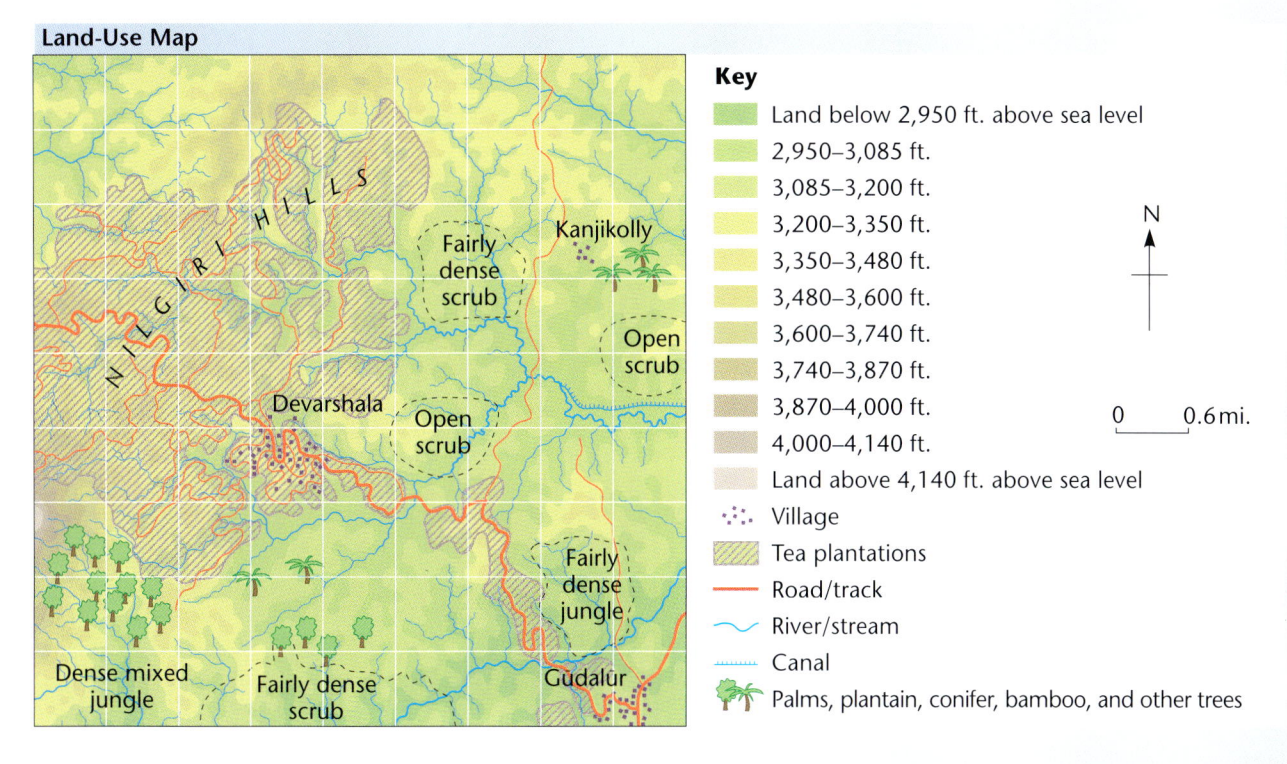

Land-Use Map

Key
- Land below 2,950 ft. above sea level
- 2,950–3,085 ft.
- 3,085–3,200 ft.
- 3,200–3,350 ft.
- 3,350–3,480 ft.
- 3,480–3,600 ft.
- 3,600–3,740 ft.
- 3,740–3,870 ft.
- 3,870–4,000 ft.
- 4,000–4,140 ft.
- Land above 4,140 ft. above sea level
- Village
- Tea plantations
- Road/track
- River/stream
- Canal
- Palms, plantain, conifer, bamboo, and other trees

FACT FILE

The Adivasi people

Most of the Adivasi people in the Nilgiri Hills live in either thatched or tiled houses in small villages. There are small local shops and tea houses in many of the villages, although one villager, Chandran from Kanjikolly, takes the bus to the nearest town of Gudalur for larger stores and services. It is 9 miles from Chandran's house to Gudalur. The road is in poor condition and very winding. The journey takes about one hour.

The Adivasi people in Chandran's village belong to three different groups, the Paniya, the Bettakurumba, and the Kattunaicken. As well as their own group's dialect, people in this area usually also speak Malaylam and Tamil, the state language. The Adivasi people have their own religious ceremonies where they pray to the spirits of the natural world around them—the trees, the sky, the plants, the water, the rocks, the earth, and the animals.

Growth of Commercial Farming in the Nilgiri Hills

Year	Area in Acres
1847	15,220
1951	112,825
1991	177,583

Chandran from Kankikolly says, "The main problem here has always been no land for the Adivasis. We've always had to fight the landlords and forestry people. Then the NGO [Non Government Organization] came and told everyone in the village what our rights were and what we could do to get our land. Now we celebrate the day when all the Adivasis of this area came together to protect our land. I'm happy my family is living here because we are all working together to make life better. We hope the youngsters will have many opportunities to do well and also be proud of being Adivasi."

4 DEVELOPMENT AND ECONOMIC GROWTH

Development in India

▶ The development of a country can be measured in two ways.

Social and economic development
One of the issues facing India is whether it can provide a good quality of life for all of its people. India has the world's largest concentration of poor people with one-third living in poverty.

DEFINITIONS OF POVERTY

There are two main definitions of poverty.

1. Relative poverty—the inequality, or gap, between the richest and poorest people, usually from the same area or country.
2. Absolute poverty—a lack of one or more of the basic requirements people need to live, such as food, shelter, or health and education services. India's definition of absolute poverty is "the lack of access to, and control over, the social economic and political resources required to meet basic human needs with dignity."

Measuring development
There are two main ways to measure development: investigating the economy and the society.

The economy
A country's **Gross National Product (GNP)** measures the wealth it creates each year. GNP per capita (per person) measures the average amount of wealth for everyone in the population. This measure is useful because it is easy to compare countries.

HOW DEVELOPMENT AFFECTS PEOPLE

Here are four Indian people talking about how development affects them.

- Sampangi says, "Without this mechanics job, I'd still be ragpicking. Now I can walk with the common people and can get married in the future."
- Nivruti Gaekwad took out a loan to buy irrigation pipes. He says, "For the first time in my life I've harvested millet in the dry season."
- Thippamma, a health worker, says, "Before I started, if there were complications with a birth, the mother had to be taken by bullock cart to the hospital eight miles away."
- Ponnuthi says, "Whether boys or girls, they should study. I'm responsible for my children, and they deserve a chance to become educated so they'll have a better future."

Countries Ranked by GNP/capita
(1997 World Bank Development Report)

Country	GNP/capita $
U.S.	28,740
Germany	28,260
Mexico	3,680
India	390
Nigeria	260

Country	Deaths per 1,000 live births
Germany	5
U.S.	7
Mexico	30
India	63
Nigeria	77

Countries Ranked by Infant Mortality Rate
(1994 World Bank Development Report)

Development and Economic Growth

There are some problems with measuring development using GNP/capita.
- It overlooks inequalities between rich and poor people.
- Some wealth is created but never measured, for example in informal jobs.
- It focuses only on money and ignores people's quality of life.

This well will provide a clean supply of water to this village. It reduces the risk of people falling ill from waterborne disease.

Social indicators

Social indicators measure people's quality of life, for example, their life expectancy and levels of health and education. They can also examine environmental quality, equality between men and women, and whether a country is democratic with guaranteed human rights. An important measure is Infant Mortality Rate (IMR), which is the number of deaths per 1000 live births. This highlights levels of health care for babies and their mothers, their diet, and also levels of education.

Social indicators give a clearer idea of people's quality of life, but can be difficult to quantify. They are also average figures, so there can be wide variation between different parts of a country or between different groups of people.

Traders at Mumbai's (Bombay's) stock market keep up-to-date with movement in the global economy.

FACT FILE

Inequality in India

Unequal access to health care. Ill-health and disease continue largely because of the lack of attention by India's leaders to poverty, illiteracy, and lack of housing. Neglect of health is shown by the paltry spending on disease prevention and health care. India's national and state governments spend about 1.3 percent of national income on health, far less than other Asian countries. This is about 2 to 3 dollars per person, not nearly enough to meet basic health needs.

India's rich and powerful people have access to world-class health care in the larger cities. Some of this care is provided inexpensively at government hospitals. High-ranking politicians can get treatment in the west at great expense, whereas, for an ordinary person, a serious illness can mean financial ruin.

Adapted from *The Financial Times*, November 8, 1994

Mother Teresa (1910–1997)

Mother Teresa, a Roman Catholic nun, devoted her life's work to India's poor and ill, and was the founder of the religious order, Missionaries of Charity. Although of Albanian descent, she became an Indian citizen in 1948. She received the Nobel Peace Price in 1979 with this citation: "The loneliest, the most wretched, and the dying has at her [Mother Teresa's] hands received compassion without condescension."

India's Industries

▶ **India's industries first developed through nationalization.**

Steel, along with other heavy industries, was one of the first industries to be nationalized by India's government after its 1947 independence.

India's growing industries

India became independent from Britain in 1947. The first Prime Minister, Jawaharlal Nehru, announced that India would "awake to life and freedom." Nehru believed that to become a success India had to develop its own industries, which had been destroyed by the British colonists.

During the 1950s the government set up and took control over, or **nationalized**, many **large-scale industries** including iron and steel, engineering, communications, and chemicals. The nationalized industries reduced the need to import goods such as steel that were important in India's development. They also created many jobs. For example, Indian state railroads employed 1.6 million people.

India's steel industry

Steel is one of India's important industries, employing almost 400,000 people. India has six major **integrated iron and steel plants** producing over 10 million tons of steel a year. The aim is to produce 33 million tons by 1999, making India the world's seventh largest producer of steel. One of the concentrations of this industry is in the state of Bihar, with production at Bokaro, Ranchi, and Jamshedpur. The advantages of a **location** in Bihar include
- good rail and road links with major centers, such as Calcutta and Patna, Bihar's state capital.
- good supplies of **raw materials** needed for steel production. Bihar accounts for 40 percent of India's iron ore production.
- good energy supplies with easy access to major coal fields.
- lots of flat land providing space for large factories.

New industries

During the 1950–1960s, new industries set up to produce **consumer goods**, such as food, drink, household goods, and cars, to be sold in India. Many of these were joint ventures with foreign firms, for example, manufacturing British cars in India. However, at that time India was not very attractive to foreign business because of strict **tariffs** and **trade barriers** that were set up to protect Indian industries from foreign competition.

In the 1960–1970s the **Green Revolution** in India's rural areas helped industries making farm equipment and fertilizers to develop.

Since the 1980s, the Indian government has reduced its controls over industry, which allowed businesses to set up more easily. Some nationalized industries have been sold off and trade restrictions reduced. This has allowed many international firms to start production in India to produce goods both for the Indian and the export markets. These firms have brought new economic growth and jobs.

Development and Economic Growth

Mohandas Gandhi is spinning cloth by hand.

Key
- --- International boundaries
- ––– State boundaries
- ○ State capital
- • Towns
- River
- Railway
- Coal
- ⊠ Iron ore
- ⊙ Steel plants

Bihar State	
Land area	67,116 sq. mi.
Population	86.34 (million)
Population density	1,272 per sq. mi.
Natural resources (coal)	with W. Bengal and Orissa, world's 4th largest reserves
Coal production	1990-91 219.3 million tons
Steel	India produced 18.5 million tons in 1993

Bihar is the center of India's steel production.

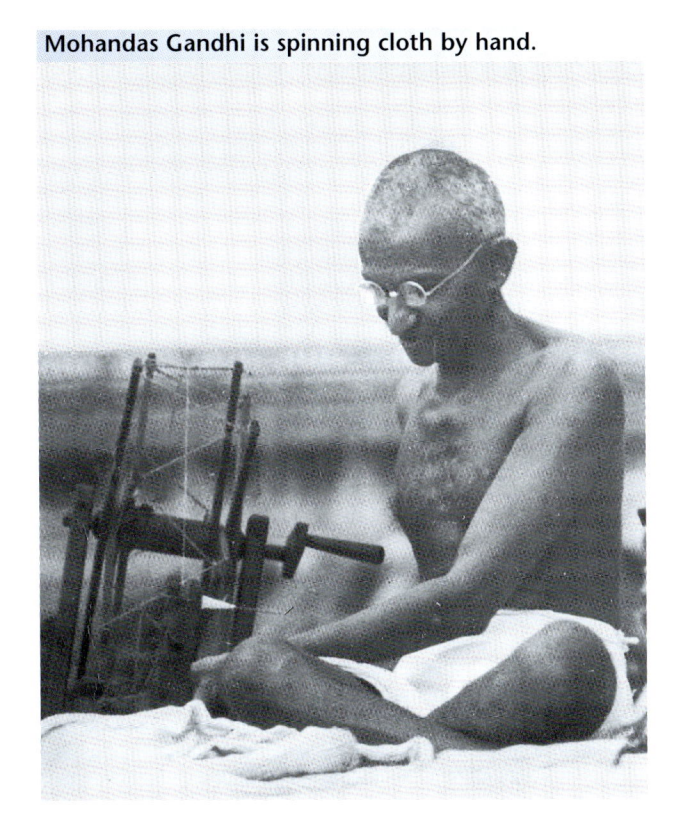

Alternatives to industrialization

Mohandas Gandhi, one of the leaders of the independence movement, criticized the path of industrial development taken by India. "How can a country with millions of living machines afford to have machines which will displace the labor of millions?" Gandhi believed development should focus on **small-scale** rural industries that would be relevant to local people's needs, for example, making farm equipment and weaving cloth. This approach is called **appropriate technology**.

FACT FILE

India's film industry

The Indian film industry is one of the largest in the world with over 700 films being made every year. About half are produced in Mumbai (Bombay). This is more films than are produced in Hollywood. Because of the size of India's film industry, Mumbai is often known as India's "Hollywood" or "Bollywood."

Many Indians go to the movies regularly, and songs from films enjoy the same popularity as pop songs in the U.S. One of India's best-known film directors is Manmohan Desai. Because of his success, he is called the "goose that lays the golden eggs." His films include the hit *Amar, Akbar, Anthony*. It follows the lives of three brothers who are separated by accident at birth and brought up by families of different faiths— Hindu, Muslim, and Christian. The brothers are finally reunited following a series of comical adventures and coincidences.

Most films are made in the Hindi language, although more are being made in regional languages. Adventure films, romances, and films about Indian society are always popular. Some film stars even become politicians.

International Companies in India

▶ International companies have a role in India's development.
▶ International companies bring advantages and disadvantages to India.

New industrial developments

Since the 1980s, many **international companies** have set up in India. International companies are businesses with offices and factories in many countries. H. D. Deve Gowda, India's former prime minister, greeted these changes saying, "We welcome foreign investment in sectors like power, tourism, ports, and **high-tech** industries."

Overseas Investment (from the U.S., EU, and Japan) in India

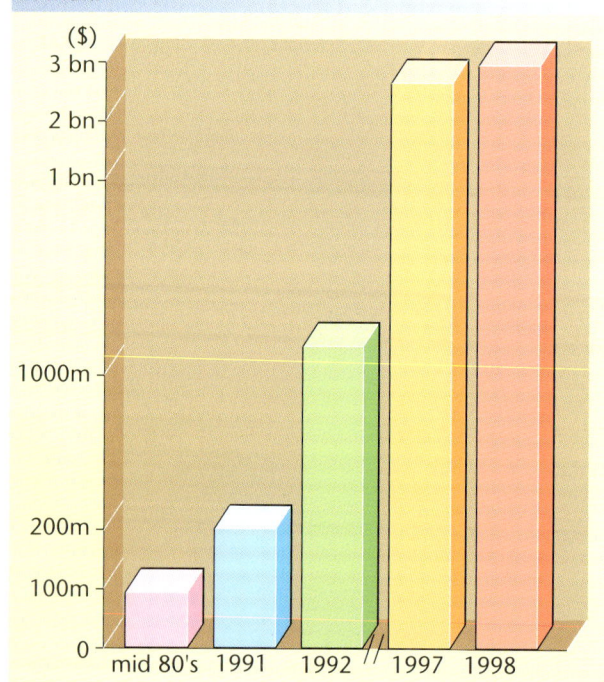

(bar chart showing investment in $: mid 80's ≈ 100m; 1991 ≈ 200m; 1992 ≈ 1000m; 1997 ≈ 3bn; 1998 ≈ 3bn)

Large numbers of overseas companies have set up in India to take advantage of low wages and India's growing demand for consumer goods. They have been helped by fewer government controls over the economy. These industries have brought many benefits to the Indian economy, for example:
- providing job opportunities
- generating tax income for India
- creating demand for Indian raw materials and power supplies
- creating demand for services and products from Indian firms
- bringing new skills and technologies into India
- producing goods for sale to both India and other countries

However, some international companies bring problems, too, for example:
- low wages
- materials imported from outside India reduce the need for materials from Indian suppliers
- environmental pollution
- **tax breaks** that encourage industries to locate in India reduce the taxes India receives from the companies
- the potential for relocation of the companies at any time because headquarters are outside India

Many of these industries also produce goods to be sold outside India, for example, sportswear, cars, and electronic goods, such as radios. This has led to changes in the pattern of India's exports as the export of manufactured goods has increased compared to India's traditional exports of agricultural produce.

Bill Gates visited India in 1997. He is the president of Microsoft, the world's largest software company.

Development and Economic Growth

Percent of Foreign Investment in India—1992

U.S.	31.7%
Switzerland	17.7%
Japan	15.7%
U.K.	3.0%
Other European countries	7.8%
Indians living abroad	11.3%
Others	12.8%

Ranking of International Companies in India

	Revenue Rs m.
Hewlitt Packard	5,780
IBM	3,560
ACER	3,200
INTEL	2,700
Digital	2,590
Compaq	2,000
Sun	1,700
Microsoft	1,120
Apple	1,100
Citizen	810

Wealth of India and the World's Six Biggest International Companies—1994

India	304 (GDP $billion)
General Motors	169 (sales $billion)
Ford	137
Toyota	111
Exxon	110
Shell	110
IBM	72

Farmers Ransack U.S. Chain in India

"Nearly 100 farmers broke through a police cordon and ransacked a Kentucky Fried Chicken outlet, demanding that the multinational fast-food leave India."

International Herald Tribune

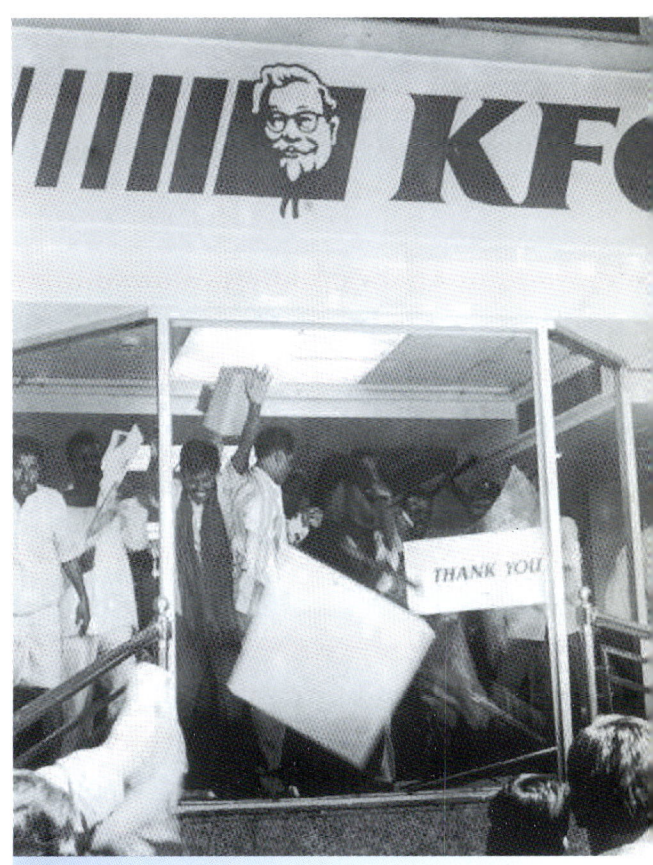

Not all multi-national firms have been welcomed by all sections of India's population. Some international companies have been accused of bringing foreign influences into India, known as "cultural imperialism," particularly from America.

FACT FILE

International companies and India's software industry

India's software industry is made up of Indian companies, international companies such as IBM, and **joint ventures** between Indian and overseas companies. India has many advantages for international companies that are trying to cut costs. For example:

- Software programmers in the U.S., Western Europe, and Japan earn about $4,000 a month, but Indian programmers are paid about $800 a month.
- India has 1.4 million software programmers, second only to the number in the U.S.
- Indian universities produce large numbers of well-educated graduates.
- When it is nighttime in North America and Europe, programmers in India can maintain western companies' software systems and process their data using high-speed satellite links.

INVESTIGATION

Economic Growth in Bangalore

▶ **Economic growth affects the city of Bangalore.**

The development of computer software is one of India's boom industries.

Bangalore—a boom town

Bangalore, in Karnartaka State, is one of India's boom cities. It has grown more than 1,000 times since independence. Its economy, based on new computer industries, is growing fast, too.

The Economist Intelligence Unit reported that "one of India's strong growth areas is computer software, where export turnover rose by 64 percent in 1995." The software industry is now worth $1.2 billion (the total IT industry being worth $2.2 billion) and much of its growth is concentrated in Bangalore, where there are more than 300 software businesses. One-third of them are owned by **international companies**, such as Hewlett Packard, IBM, and Digital.

Today electrical engineering employs over 7 percent of the total workforce of Bangalore, with 10,000 people working in **high-tech** businesses.

Why has Bangalore become so successful?

- Historical tradition: Bangalore has a tradition of high-tech industries. Many government research companies were already located in this area, such as India Telecom Industries, Hindustan Machine Tools, and the India Space Research Organization.
- An educated and skilled work force: There are many colleges, universities, and research institutes, which train people to work in high-tech industries.
- Good communications: Bangalore has an airport and advanced satellite communications, which allow quick communications with firms in Europe and America.
- Government support: The State government encourages high-tech industries by creating business parks and services.
- Quality of life: The cooler climate and large number of parks and green areas give Bangalore its name of "India's Garden City." The development of Bangalore "took off because of the quality of people and the quality of life," said Namdan Nilakeni, founder of Infosys Technologies, one of Bangalore's largest companies.

In addition to jobs and wealth, economic growth has also brought traffic congestion and pollution.

Development and Economic Growth

THE UPSIDE AND DOWNSIDE OF GROWTH

Dilip D'Souza of *New Internationalist* said, "Software has certainly brought prosperity to thousands of people, but there is a down side too." Bangalore has grown very quickly, so there is a housing shortage. Large numbers of people live in slum dwellings, and the city's electricity, water, and sewage services struggle to keep up with the pressures placed on them. The airport was designed to cater for 700 people a day and now struggles to cope with 6,000 a day. The streets are often congested with Bangalore's 850,000 vehicles. City garbage is often uncleared; water is getting scarce; traffic is a nightmare; public transportation is hopelessly inadequate and house prices are beyond the reach of ordinary people."

India's Computer Industry in Bangalore

Computer Industry

India's computing industry has grown rapidly over the last 15 years, with Bangalore in Southern India becoming the "electronics capital" of the country. Many multinational companies have established bases in India. These provide 24-hour a day online software support at a fraction of the cost of paying shift workers in Europe or the U.S. Companies that are currently using India for offshore support include Abbey National, North West Water, Reuters, and Avis Europe.

In addition, there are over 700 software companies in India, employing more than 140,000 people. Computer hardware and electronic components are also manufactured in India. These firms earn 80–90% of their income from exports, but India's internal computer-based services remain undeveloped.

India is attractive for foreign computer companies like IBM, Microsoft, Texas Instruments, and Compaq because overall costs are about 50% of those in the West. Wages especially are lower than those in the U.S. and Europe, making it cheaper for companies to employ experienced and talented people. However, because reliable electricity supplies and communication networks are often not available locally, hi-tech companies have to provide these facilities themselves, increasing their costs.

Global Eye, Issue 4, Autumn 1997

Changing Employment in Bangalore

	Electronics % of employees	Textiles % of employees
1941	0.0	12.0
1951	1.0	14.6
1961	2.8	13.7
1971	6.0	10.5
1981	6.8	8.0
1991	8.0	7.0

FACT FILE

The IT industry

The IT (information technology) industry is one of India's success stories. In 1996 the software industry was growing by about 50 percent a year, with 40 percent of sales in India and 60 percent for export. For example, when trains on the London subways run on time, or American Airlines planes take off safely, it is partly thanks to software designed in India. The two charts to the right tell more of India's software story. The first chart ranks India's cities by their percentages of the entire Indian software industry. The second chart shows where in the word the software is going.

India's software cities	
Mumbai (Bombay)	34%
Bangalore	26%
Delhi	20%
Pune	6%
Calcutta	5%
Others	9%

Software exports 1996	
U.S.	57%
Europe	22%
Asia	13%
Others	8%

INVESTIGATION

Tourism in Goa

▶ Tourism has an impact.
▶ Economic changes affect people.

Goa is a delightful place beside the Arabian Sea, with golden beaches, gleaming whitewashed houses, and perhaps the friendliest people in India.

Why do people visit Goa?

Tourists are attracted to Goa by its natural resources, local culture, traditions, and services built for tourism. These include

- its 65 miles of sandy, palm-fringed beaches.
- hot, dry weather in the tourist season with ten hours of daily sunshine.
- flights to Dabolim Airport.
- tourist hotels on the beaches.

Tourism has brought many advantages to Goa, such as

- construction jobs to build hotels.
- jobs in hotels and other services.
- improved communications systems.
- income from tourism, such as from selling handicrafts.

But the coast is a fragile environment. In places like Goa, where many people visit one small area, tourism can have a negative impact on the local people and the environment.

Goa's coastline of white sands and palms provides an ideal location for a beach vacation.

Goa is located on India's western coast. It was once a **colony** of Portugal, so its culture is a mixture of Indian and Portuguese traditions. The sea, beach, and coastal sand dunes support the livelihoods of local people through fishing, farming, and tapping **toddy**. Toddy is a drink made from palm tree juice. In the last 30 years Goa has developed as a major tourist destination.

Number of Visiting Tourists

Year	Number of Tourists
1972	10,000
1990	1,000,000
2000	5,000,000 (estimate)

Major Tourist Sites in Goa

Key
- Major hotel complexes
- Main tourist beaches
- Towns and villages
- Bridges providing road access

Development and Economic Growth

In ten years Goa will be just one long strip of hotels indistinguishable from Thailand, Miami Beach, or Benidorm. . . . we should find somewhere else to go, with a culture that is not fragile and with very little of value that can be damaged.

Clive Anderson, BBC film *Our Man in Goa*

Climate Data for Goa

The Downside of Tourism

What problems does tourism create?

Many of the changes brought by tourism affect local people's way of life. For example, sand dunes have been cleared to provide space for hotel lawns, raising fears of increased beach erosion. Some hotels have closed off access to the beach, preventing people getting access for fishing. Hotels also have a big impact on local services.

- A tourist in a 5-star hotel uses 28 times more electricity than a local person.
- One hotel can use as much water as five villages.
- Some hotels get water from illegal wells, cutting local farmers' water supply.

FACT FILE

Tourism Concern

The increase in tourism around the world has brought new prosperity to many areas. It has also often damaged the environment and the area's traditional way of life. Hotels and tourist accommodations have been built without consideration for their surroundings. Tourists use much greater quantities of electricity and water than the local people in their own houses, sometimes causing shortages. The effect of great numbers of people on delicate environments, such as coral reefs, has been devastating.

Tourism Concern is a charity aiming to promote greater understanding of the impact of tourism on host communities and environments. Its work in Goa has highlighted some of the negative impacts of tourism on this region of India. A Tourism Concern report argued that,

"Goan people are asking why they can no longer afford the high prices of some of the traditional food like fish and cashew nuts. A local women's group is protesting how they are portrayed in the tourism literature and why they and the local carnival are being turned into a show at the expense of their dignity and culture. They are also asking why their children prefer to skip school and become involved in selling goods, often drugs, to tourists. They ask why tourists continue to insult the morality of local residents by continuing to sunbathe in the nude."

5 REGIONAL AND NATIONAL DEVELOPMENT

Regional Inequalities in India

▶ **Development is not evenly spread across India.**

There are many differences in the quality of life between India's rural and urban areas. There are also differences in the quality of life across India's regions. The physical geography of many regions, such as the mountains of Kashmir or the desert areas of Rajasthan, present difficulties for development (see pages 32–33). In other areas, economic policies have led to high rates of economic growth. For example, Bangalore has encouraged business development. **Adult literacy** is one of the key measures of development and the pattern across India is shown on the map to the right.

"There are some poles of economic growth, notably the western states of Maharashtra (including Bombay), and Gujarat, as well as Harayana, Punjab, Goa, and Karnataka (including Bangalore). There is a concentration of poverty in northern and eastern regions of Bihar, Orissa, and eastern Uttar Pradesh."

The Economist Magazine

Indian Literacy Rates in 1991

Key % of population
- More than 64%
- 52–64%
- National average 52%
- 40–52%
- Under 40%
- Figures not available

Development in Kerala

One region that has achieved many development successes is the state of Kerala in southwest India. It is a very fertile area of India and a mainly agricultural state. The population density is high with 76 percent of people living in rural areas, especially in the flat land along the coast. Inland are the steep slopes of the Western Ghats. In Kerala many farmers own their land, unlike many other states in India.

The Kerala state government has an approach to development that makes people's **basic needs** and quality of life the first priority. The state government aims for the whole population to have good levels of health care and education. It has provided subsidized food and social security, free school meals for school children, and literacy classes for adults. For example, villages have a **ration shop** selling food and fuel at government controlled prices. According to K. P. Kannan, professor of development studies, "Kerala has targeted the most vulnerable among the poor, such as destitute, pregnant women, children, and the elderly."

Regional and National Development

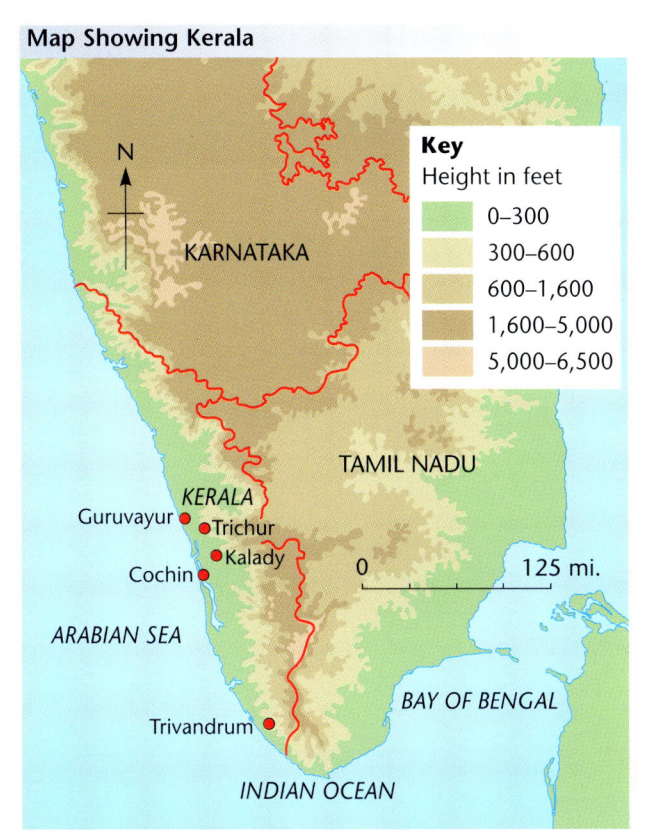

Map Showing Kerala

Key
Height in feet
- 0–300
- 300–600
- 600–1,600
- 1,600–5,000
- 5,000–6,500

Kerala is not a wealthy state, but it has achieved important successes. Infant Mortality is a third lower and its literacy levels 30 percent higher than in the Punjab, although the Punjab is a much richer state with incomes far higher than India's national average. As Binu S. Thomas, researcher for ACTIONAID-India, says, "Kerala has achieved for its 30 million people (a population the size of Canada) a quality of life comparable to the developed world in life expectancy, literacy, population growth, and infant mortality."

	Health—beds/1,000 people	Female literacy rates	Income per person as % of national average
Kerala	44/1,000	87%	84%
Punjab (Thar Desert)	16/1,000	49%	176%
Karnataka (Bangalore)	9/1,000	44%	85%

Regional Development Statistics

FACT FILE

Kerala

Kerala is one of the most densely populated, culturally mixed, and politically unusual states in the world.
- It supports a population of 29 million people.
- Its population is 60 percent Hindu, 20 percent Muslim, and 20 percent Christian.
- In 1957 Kerala was the first state to vote a communist government to power by democratic elections.
- More than 90 percent of people in Kerala own the land on which their home stands.
- Coir (coconut fiber) accounts for 18 percent of exports and supports 10 million people in Kerala.
- Its major exports include rubber, spices, coffee, tea, and cashew nuts.
- An estimated 150,000 Kerala people work in the Gulf states. They are known as "gulfen." Many are skilled technicians and medical staff. The money they send home makes an important contribution to the economy

The New Internationalist

People in Kerala live longer, thanks to better nutrition and state health care provision. Far fewer children die in their first year.

	Life expectancy (years)	Infant mortality (per 1,000 births)
Kerala	70	20
India	56	94
U.S.	75	10

People Involved in India's Development

▶ **Many people are involved in India's development.**

A wide range of people and organizations are involved in India's development. They include
- India's people.
- 50,000 Indian community development organizations, often called nongovernment organizations (NGOs).
- India's businesses.
- local, state, and national governments.
- aid-giving countries.
- international NGOs.
- international organizations such as the World Bank and **International Monetary Fund**.

When investigating development, it is important to start from local people's thinking. Local people have experience of the conditions and often already know ways of responding to the problems they face. For example, in 1974 the women of Reni in northern India stopped loggers from cutting down 4,600 square miles of forest by hugging trees. It was the start of the **Chipko** environmental movement. Professor Bina Agarwal said, "On one occasion the Chipko women prevented the axing of an oak forest to establish a potato farm for men. This would have added five miles to the women's journey to collect fuel wood, while the money from the potatoes would have remained with the men."

Embracing trees, members of the Chipko movement prevent trees from being felled by loggers.

The Chipko movement helped to slow down the destruction of forests and forced the Indian government to pass environmental protection laws. The movement has won many awards and has been copied elsewhere in the world.

URMUL Trust

URMUL Trust is an Indian NGO established in 1984. It is based in the desert state of Rajasthan where it runs health, education, drought relief, and rural development work. It works with more than 4,000 families and spends almost 50 percent of its income on supporting local community groups. These groups organize a number of activities including cooperative businesses and legal aid.

This women's community group in the Nilgiri Hills is supported by the charity ACTIONAID. The women are discussing their problems and identifying ways of overcoming them.

Types of aid
As well as India's own achievements, there is also international support for development through aid. There are different forms of aid.
- Bilateral aid from one country to another.
- Multilateral aid from international organizations such as the World Bank.
- Voluntary aid from development charities such as Oxfam and ACTIONAID.
- Other forms of aid from military assistance or technological support.

United States government aid to India
The United States government budgeted a total of $144.5 million in aid to India for the fiscal year beginning October 1999. The total amount of the aid is divided into the following allocations:
- development assistance—$56.5 million
- food assistance—$88 million

An additional $450,000 was also allocated for international military education and training.

ACTIONAID—an international NGO
ACTIONAID has operated in India since 1972. This organization works with more than one million people and spends $2.5 million a year. It works by providing funds and support to local Indian NGOs, such as the URMUL Trust, so it can achieve "the empowerment of the poor in the process of social development." ACTIONAID also shares its experience with others involved in development, both within India and internationally. For example, in 1996 Amitava Mukherjee, ACTIONAID-India's director, said that the planned United Nations Food Summit, "should be renamed the World Summit on Hunger to focus attention on the urgent need to eliminate hunger and food insecurity." Most of ACTIONAID's money is given by members of the public.

FACT FILE
Two ways of looking at development
The Narmada River project to bring water to a desert region of Gujarat in northwest India shows that not everybody agrees on the best path to development. The Narmada project has been planned since 1947. There are 30 large dams, 135 medium dams, and 3,000 small dams planned for irrigation, water supply, and hydroelectric power.

The world's largest irrigation dam, the Sardar Sarovar Dam, is to be completed by the year 2000. It will bring piped water to all 5,614 villages and 130 towns in the region at a cost of $52.5 million. The building of the dam, originally funded with loans from the World Bank, employs 7,000 local people.

For many people, the project represents progress towards a modern India. Other Indians disagree, and many demonstrations against the dam have been held by community groups and Indian environmental organizations. They oppose the dam because it will flood farmland, villages, and forests. They support smaller projects. Thousands of local people have been forcibly removed and thousands more will be displaced when the dam is complete.

This pattern is repeated across India, where dams planned or under construction will mean that more than 700,000 people are displaced. Community and environmental groups argue that the money could be better spent on smaller projects based on the needs of local communities. The conflict is whether the best path to development is through modernization or through grassroots development.

The New Internationalist and *Understanding Global Issues*

India's Changing Economy

▶ **Economic changes bring wealth and poverty.**

This car factory was funded by a joint venture between Indian and Korean producers.

Changing employment

In the last fifty years there have been major changes in the type of jobs Indian people do. While jobs in farming are still very important, urbanization and industrialization have led to the growth of **secondary** and **tertiary employment**.

Changes in the Economy—% of Wealth Created (GDP)

Sector	1950	1960	1970	1980	1990	1996
Primary	55	46	45	38	32	29
Secondary	15	21	22	26	28	29
Tertiary	30	33	33	36	40	42

India's successes

In the 1980s and 1990s India made changes to the economy to make it easier for new industries to set up. Many new industries produced **consumer** products for sale to people in India and for export. Many industries were set up with the help of **international companies** based in Europe or the U.S. These changes led to high rates of economic growth, more than 5 percent a year, and increased foreign investment in the economy. Rent for **commercial** property in Mumbai (Bombay) is now more expensive than in New York.

The growth of these industries has led to changes in the pattern of India's **imports** and **exports**. In the past, India imported many goods, but its exports were small. Recently, exports grew by about 7 percent a year, but imports grew by 3 percent. This is because more consumer goods are produced by India's own industries, so there is less need for imports.

Mumbai (Bombay) docks is the site where much of India's importing and exporting take place.

Regional and National Development

The downside

To help industry grow, India had to spend more money buying oil from overseas. Things were made worse when the price of oil doubled in the 1970s and rose again in 1990. As a result, India's **external debt**—the money it owes to other countries—leaped from $20 billion in 1980 to $90 billion in 1990. This debt costs India a huge amount of money every year. In 1994 the debt payments were 27 percent of the value of India's exports.

To pay for this debt, India had to take out a large loan from the **International Monetary Fund (IMF)**. In return for this money, India agreed to change the structure of its economy. This **Structural Adjustment Plan (SAP)** meant the government had to take less part in running the economy and leave more decisions to business people. To do this, the government
- **privatized** or sold off state-owned business.
- reduced export tariffs and taxes.
- allowed more international companies to start new businesses in India.
- reduced government **subsidies** on some goods and cut back some services.
- cut "**red tape**," to allow easier imports and exports.

These changes helped improve the economy for businesses, but they affected the poorest people badly. India does provide a safety net to support its poorest people through health and education services and, for example, by subsidizing food and goods at certain shops.

However, the economic changes of the SAP led to cuts in jobs, wages, and the government's safety net. Increased food prices have affected the people's ability to provide for themselves.

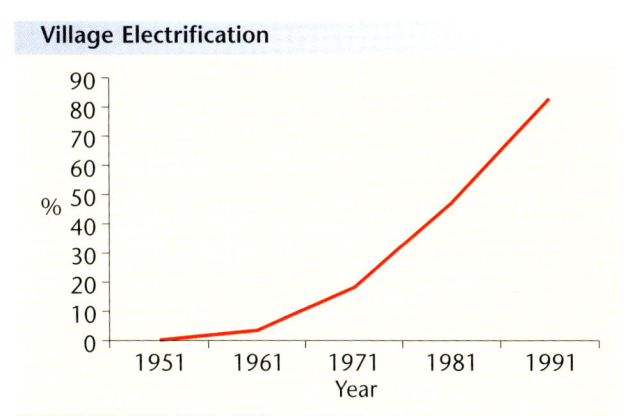

Village Electrification

% of People Living Below the Poverty Line

Year	Rural	Urban	Total
1983	40.4	28.1	37.5
1988	22.5	14.2	20.4
1990	19.7	10.8	17.4
1992	22.9	13.0	20.3
1994	21.7	11.6	19.0

Vehicle Sales

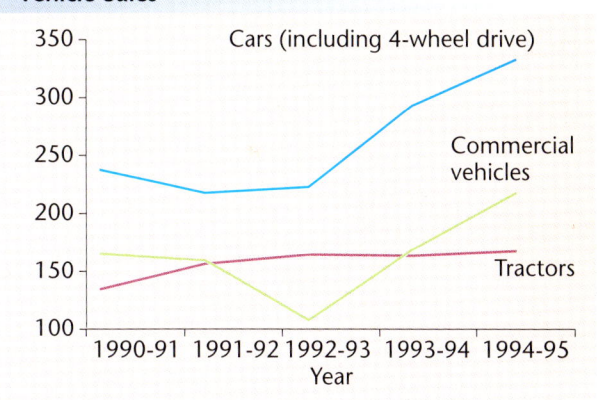

Three Statistics Giving Evidence of Economic Changes

FACT FILE

India's changing steel industry

India's steel industry has several advantages. It has all the major raw materials needed for a modern steel industry including
- 12 billion tons of good quality iron ore, enough to last 160 years.
- 8 billion tons of coaking coal, enough to last 100 years.
- large amounts of limestone and manganese ore.
- a skilled workforce.

Its seven large integrated steel plants and nearly 200 smaller furnaces have been protected from foreign competition by high taxes on imports.

Many plants are outdated and inefficient. The government is reducing controls and encouraging modernization and expansion.

Crude Steel Production	
	million tons
1950/51	1.50
1960/61	3.42
1970/71	6.30
1980/81	9.39
1990/91	14.92
1999/2000	35.00

United Nations Industrial Development Organization

Development Trends in India

▶ **People's lives are improving in India.**

Fifty years of progress

Despite the many problems facing India, it has made great strides in development. One of the key signs of progress is that India is now self-sufficient in food and often exports food grains. Only 50 years ago millions of people were affected by famine, and India had to rely on food aid from foreign countries.

Over the same period India has established itself as the world's largest democratic country. This allows people to freely express their views about changes taking place in their country and hold their leaders accountable at elections. As *The Economist* magazine reported, "Although literacy levels are low, villagers throughout India discuss politics with great enthusiasm. But they are also doubtful about the promises given to them before each election and use their votes carefully."

How does this affect people?

These changes affect individuals, as well as countries. A villager from Asegaon village said, "That's my well and where I grow vegetables. They are a priority because I can feed my family and sell what's left over. Before this, my children hardly knew the taste of vegetables."

The general increase in people's wealth can be seen in the growing demand for consumer goods in India. In 1994 Indians owned more than 77 million bicycles, 40 million TVs, and 64 million radios to name just a few products. Other improvements can be seen in the chart on the next page.

This is a polling booth in Delhi during India's recent general election.

Regional and National Development

Does economic development improve the quality of life?

India's Development Achievements

Literacy Rate*

	1951(%)	1995(%)
Total	20	52
Men	27	64
Women	9	36

(* India now has over 10 million university graduates)

Infant Mortality Rate

1947	1960	1995
270/1,000	144/1,000	70/1,000

Life Expectancy

1947	1995
27 years	62 years

It should not be forgotten that almost 30 percent of India's population still live below the government's poverty line, and in 1990, 40 percent of the world's poorest people lived in India.

1977	78,305 million
1987	88,240 million
1993	94,169 million

People Living in Poverty

Whatever the approach, the important question should always be, "How is the quality of people's lives affected?" For example, as the economy grows, more wealth is created, but the question is, "How is it shared by different groups in society?"

> "There is evidence that economic growth does not always improve the quality of life. The environmental destruction and loss of livelihoods caused by mining and major irrigation projects have done more harm than good to the quality of life of the poor, regardless of rises in GNP."
>
> Binu S. Thomas, ACTIONAID-India

FACT FILE

Democracy

Since independence in 1947, democracy has become firmly embedded in Indian society. Every time India holds a general election it enters the Guinness Book of Records for sending the most voters to the polls. In 1991, more than 514 million Indians cast their votes, about four times the number of voters in India's first election after independence in 1952.

Indian elections are on such a scale that it takes several days to count all the votes. To ensure that all those eligible can vote, whether they can read or not, each party has a symbol which voters recognize and mark their vote next to. For example, the Congress Party uses a hand held in greeting, and the Lok Dal, a party which draws votes from agricultural workers, uses the image of two cows and a farmer plowing. India's first democratically elected Prime Minister was Jawaharlal Nehru, who led India from 1947 to 1964. His party, the Congress Party, has held power for most of the period since independence.

The Congress Party is one of the world's oldest political parties. But there are numerous other political parties in India, representing different regional, religious, class, and political groupings. In contrast, the colors of the Indian flag represent unity: Saffron yellow is the color of Hinduism and Buddhism, green is the color of Islam, and the wheel of life is in the center.

6 INDIA'S FUTURE

India and the Global Community

▶ **India has yet to follow the Asian Tigers.**

Despite India's huge size, it only accounts for just under 1 percent of world trade. India's recent economic changes have increased the amount of its manufactured **exports**, such as electronic goods. Other Asian countries have also been developing their manufacturing industries, particularly Hong Kong (now part of China), Taiwan, Singapore, and South Korea. These four countries, known as the Asian Tigers, have built very successful economies based on the export of manufactured products. They have quickly moved from relatively poor nations to what are known as **Newly Industrialized Countries (NICS)**.

Access to overseas markets

Many people have wondered whether India could match their success. As Manmohan Singh, India's Minister of Finance in 1991, said "Why does everyone talk about South Korea? This is because in 1960, South Korea had the same income per person as India. Today, South Korea's income is ten times India's!"

Airfreight provides rapid access for Indian goods to get to the global market.

One of the problems for the NICs, and also for India, is whether they can get access to overseas markets where they can sell their products. More countries are joining up to form trading blocs such as the **European Union (EU)** and the North American Trade Association (NAFTA). It is often difficult for countries like India to gain access to these markets. For example, India's export of textiles to America increased by 65 percent during the early 1990s, but in the future, NAFTA may restrict India's exports. A representative from

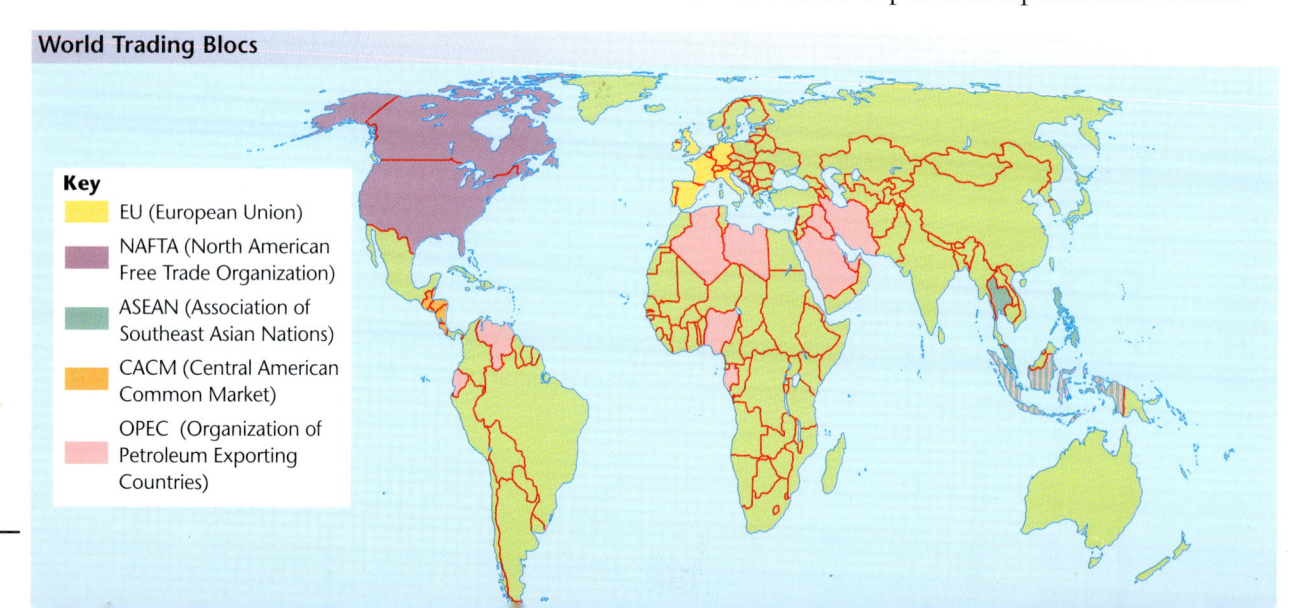

World Trading Blocs

Key
- EU (European Union)
- NAFTA (North American Free Trade Organization)
- ASEAN (Association of Southeast Asian Nations)
- CACM (Central American Common Market)
- OPEC (Organization of Petroleum Exporting Countries)

the American Textile Manufacturers says, "We see NAFTA as very positive because it can reduce the Asian imports."

The demand for some exports, such as basic electrical goods, produced by the NICs is also limited. The NICs have been able to overcome this by producing new goods such as **high-tech** equipment. This process is starting in Bangalore (see pages 42–43).

Some people do not believe that the low wages paid to workers in many manufacturing industries will be good enough for long term economic growth. Mr. Dang from Hindustani Computers says, "Low salaries are not going to sustain growth. What is going to count is professional competence, using our skills and technology."

CHARACTERISTICS OF NICS

- Manufacturing production is growing fast—mainly for export
- Few government controls in the economy
- Low wages
- Education and training very important
- Small farming sector with less than 10 percent income from agriculture
- Population and population growth less than 1.5 percent.

% of Proportion of World Trade

	1970	1990
EU	48	43
U.S.	13	15
Japan	10	13
Developing countries	4.5	10
India	0.5	1
Newly industrialized countries	4	9
Others	20	12

% of Distribution of India's exports—1994–95

U.S.	19
Japan	8
Germany	7
U.K.	6
Russia	3
France	2
Other developed countries	16
OPEC	9
Eastern Europe	4
Developing countries	24
Others	4

% of Total of India's Imports and Exports—1991

	Imports	Exports
Total (Million $s)	19,509	17,900
Food/live animals	2.0	15.2
Drinks/tobacco	0.0	0.9
Crude materials/non–food	7.7	7.2
Mineral fuels, lubricants, etc.	30	2.4
Animal/vegetable oils/ fats	0.7	0.4
Chemicals	15.8	8.4
Manufactured goods	19.4	37.5
Machinery/transportation equipment	13.5	7.5
Misc. manufactured goods	2.9	19.0
Misc. transactions and goods	8.0	1.6

FACT FILE
A changing world order

Developing World to Eclipse Europe says World Bank

The Big Five developing countries—Brazil, China, India, Indonesia, and Russia—will transform the world economic map over the next 25 years as they first catch up and then overtake Europe in terms of global trade, a report from the World Bank claims.

The Bank is upbeat about the prospects for developing countries—including those who have experienced declining rather than rising standards in recent years. It forecasts that the economies of developing countries as a whole will grow twice as fast between now and 2006. In 1913 developing countries accounted for 16.5 percent of the world's total Gross Domestic Product. By 1995 this has grown to 18 percent and is projected to reach 33 percent by the year 2020.

The Daily Telegraph September 10, 1997

The Prospects for India's Development

▶ **India's development faces difficulties and challenges.**

You have seen many of the challenges facing India's development prospects, including
- its monsoon climate (pages 10–11).
- the size and diversity of its population (pages 16–19).
- the size of India's debt (pages 50–51).
- high rates of poverty (pages 36–37).
- high rates of rural-urban migration (pages 20–21).

India faces other challenges, too.

Historical

After almost 200 years of extracting India's wealth, by exporting its raw materials or selling British goods to its people, British power was handed over to India in 1947. The British left behind a farming system that could not feed its people, few industries, and a population with low levels of education and health.

At the end of British rule, India was divided into two countries. India became a largely Hindu nation, and a new Muslim state, Pakistan, was founded. This created massive disruption as 15 million people moved from one country to another. It also created friction between India and Pakistan, leading to a number of armed conflicts. Distrust continues between the two countries today.

Social problems

From time to time there is tension between India's different religions. For example in 1992, a dispute between Hindus and Muslims over the situation of a mosque and temple at Ayodhya turned into rioting throughout India. India has also suffered tension in some of its own states such as Kashmir.

Water supply

More irrigation has provided better water supplies for many farmers, but in places too much water has been **extracted** so the level of **underground water** has been lowered. The United Nations has reported that India's ground water is being extracted faster than it is being **recharged**.

To increase water supplies in the area around Calcutta, India has built a barrier across the Ganges River at Farakka. But the Ganges River also flows through Bangladesh, which means there is less water for irrigation and drinking for people there.

Deforestation

Only 6.5 percent of rural households have electricity, so people need another source of fuel for heating and cooking. The most common fuel in rural areas is wood and this has placed great demands on forests. India's forests are also under threat from logging and other forms of exploitation.

A train is taking Muslims to the new Muslim country of Pakistan, which was created by the partition of India in 1947.

India's Future

Deforestation leads to high rates of soil erosion in parts of the Himalayas.

THE SHRINKING FORESTS OF INDIA

Concern is growing about India's forests, which shrank at a rate of 0.6 percent during the 1980s.

Agricultural land has suffered as the fertile soil is washed away. Deforestation is blamed for flash floods, inadequate recharging of underground water supplies, and silted-up rivers.

Financial Times September 6, 1995

Natural disasters

"Natural disasters in India have included rampaging floods, when rivers extended their watery grip over large areas of land, and scorching droughts, which have left behind festering sores on once fertile lands."

The Indian Center for Science and Environment

FACT FILE

Transportation

India is a very large country and needs a network of roads and railroads to transport goods and people hundreds of miles every day. The road system is still in need of considerable improvement. Over 60,000 people are killed on India's roads each year.

"Although the rail and postal systems are quite impressive, and ports, air services, and telecommunications are improving, roads are generally quite unsuited to modern requirements. While India has about one-half million miles of surfaced roads, more than one-third of villages have no road link and 70 percent have no "all-weather" links. The quality of roads, even the national highways, is generally appalling by international standards. They are narrow, badly maintained, highly congested, slow, and dangerous. The number of vehicles has risen from 300,000 in 1950/51 to 31 million in 1995/96."

The Economist, 1997

Only a small portion of the population owns cars. The vast majority travel by bus or train. More than ten million travel on India's 38,600 miles of rail network every day. There are still some steam locomotives in use, and the longest journey of 2,318 miles from Jammu in the north to Kanya Kumari in the south takes 89 hours.

India's Future

▶ India's future is yet to be shaped.

A family in Rajasthan prepares for their son's marriage.

Fifty years ago India was ruled by a colonial power, had few industries of its own, and was barely able to feed itself. Today, India has made huge improvements in the quality of life for its people.

> "In its industrial and technological achievements, it is arguably a giant. Its industrial expertise extends into such advanced fields as nuclear energy, satellites, and software design."

The Economist Magazine

Many influences will shape India's future. These include decolonization, democracy, and tourism.

DECOLONIZATION

Many colonial names for places are being changed, such as Bombay, where *bombaim*—Portuguese for a good harbor—became the English word *Bombay*. The new Indian name is Mumbai. According to Sushila Singh, "The changes are a way for people to show their Indianess by getting rid of the colonial legacy."

DEMOCRACY

India has remained as a democratic country for more than 50 years. Democracy is important because it allows people to express ideas openly, debate them, vote for their own government, and hold their politicians accountable to the people.

TOURISM

Two million tourists a year visit India bringing $1.5 billion into the economy. Tourists range from backpackers, getting by on a few dollars a day, to those booking 5-star hotels. However, *The Economist* magazine reported that "India has barely tapped its vast tourism potential with under 0.4 percent of the world's tourists and about 1 percent of tourist spending." To encourage tourism, new hotels have been built, more international flights scheduled, and better communications have been developed.

India's Future

So what will the future bring?

From the pastoral farmers of the Thar Desert to Bangalore's bustling computer factories, the people of India are working to improve their quality of life.

However, there are many human and physical geographical processes that influence how these changes affect India's people.

India has successfully launched its own satellites, and high-tech industries are well-established.

FACT FILE

India in a high-tech age

"In the last decade or so the Eastern Tiger economies leapfrogged over the stage of industrial development and pushed into the information age. Singapore, for example, has the world's most sophisticated telecommunications infrastructure and is a center for multinational computer firms. Hong Kong's rule in global finance equals that of London or New York. Singapore is a world leader in manufacturing sophisticated, **high-tech** quality products.

As we move towards the 21st century, Asia will become the dominant region of the world technologically, economically, politically, culturally, and militarily. Until the 1990s, the West set their own rules for the Asians; this is no longer so. Asians are creating their own rules."

Dr. Amitava Mukherjee, Director, ACTIONAID-India

India's place in future world population

India's population in 1947, when it gained independence, was 350 million people. Fifty years later the population is nearly one billion at 975,800,000. Although India's population growth rate has slowed down due to a family-planning policy, the projection for India's population in 2050 is that it will be the world's most populous country, followed by China, Pakistan, the United States, and Nigeria.

Map of India

More Books to Read

Cumming, David. *The Ganges Delta & Its People.* Chatham, NJ: Raintree Steck-Vaughn. 1994.

Cumming David. *The Ganges.* Chatham, NJ: Raintree Steck-Vaughn. 1993.

Dhanjal, Beryl. *Amritsar.* Parsippany, NJ: Silver Burdett Press. 1994.

Ganeri Anita. *India.* Danbury, CT: Franklin Watts. 1994.

Howard, Dale E. *India.* Minneapolis, MN: Children's Press. 1996.

Kadodwala, Dilip. *Hinduism.* Chatham, NJ: Raintree Steck-Vaughn Publishers. 1995.

Nugent, Nicholas. *India.* Chatham, NJ: Raintree Steck-Vaughn Publishers. 1991.

Penney, Sue. *Sikhism.* Chatham, NJ: Raintree Steck-Vaughn. 1996.

Prior, Katherine. *Indian Subcontinent.* Danbury, CT: Franklin Watts. 1997.

Streissguth, Thomas. *India.* Minneapolis, MN: Lerner Publishing Group. 1998.

Glossary

adult literacy the number of people who can read and write per 1000 of the population

alluvial a type of fine mud or silt deposited by rivers

altitude(s) height above sea level

appropriate technology the use of **small-scale**, simple tools which are more useful to people in rural areas

basic needs things like food, shelter, and health care

birth rate number of live births per 1000 of the population

castes a system of social groups into which people are born. Traditionally castes were associated with particular jobs.

central business district (CBD) the central part of a town or city containing offices and stores

Chipko an environmental movement that started when Indian women began to "hug" trees to prevent them from being cut down

collision plate margin where two plates collide or push together causing massive earthquakes

colony a country that is under the control of a more powerful one

commercial for use by businesses

common land land used by everyone in a community, such as land used for grazing

consumer person who buys and uses a product

consumer goods items for direct sale to the public

crust the earth's outer layer. Below the earth's crust, the rocks are in a semi-molten state.

Glossary, continued

death rate number of deaths per 1000 of population

earthquake unpredictable movements in the earth, which cause the ground to shake, and which can be strong enough to destroy buildings

economically active the people within a country's population who are of working age

EU (European Union) the group of 15 countries that work together to improve their trade, economic, social, and environmental policies

eroded the result when top soil is removed through the action of water or wind

export the sale of goods produced in one country to another country

external debt the amount owed to other countries

extracted removed or taken out of

farm labor the actual work on the farm

fertilizers any material used to enrich and fertilize soil

fold mountains when two plates collide, the land between them is forced upwards to form fold mountains

food crops crops, such as wheat or rice, that are grown for people to eat

Green Revolution a series of changes that took place in Indian agriculture using a high technology approach, such as the use of chemical fertilizers and **high yielding varieties (HYV)** of crops, to increase crop production

Gross Domestic Product (GDP) the market value of all goods and services that have been bought for final use in a period of time

Gross National Product (GNP) a measure of the amount of wealth produced by a country each year. GNP/capita shows the average amount of goods and services each person within a country creates.

ground water water found below the surface in a permeable rock

high-tech high technology

high yielding varieties (HYVs) new types of crops that have been scientifically developed to produce a greater harvest

imports goods and services coming into a country

informal settlements areas where people, often new migrants in an urban area, have built homes on land without permission

integrated iron and steel plants both types of manufacturing in one location

international companies companies with headquarters in other countries

International Monetary Fund (IMF) an organization set up to help countries' economies

large-scale industries where many people are employed in many locations

location where an industry or firm is set up

migrants people who have moved from one place to another, such as from a rural to an urban area

migrations the movement of people (or animals) from one place to another

monsoon the season that brings the main rains to India

mountain chain range of mountains linked together

nationalized industries which are owned and run by a country's government

natural increase the increase in population caused by the difference between the birth and death rate

Newly Industrialized Countries (NICs) a group of countries in Asia that have moved relatively quickly from being less-developed nations to having successful economies based on the export of manufactured products

peri-urban growth the growth of settlements on the edges of urban areas. These settlements often have both rural and urban characteristics.

pesticides chemical substances used to kill insects or animals that are seen as harmful to people or crops

plantations large estates on which crops, such as tea or coffee, are grown for sale

plates the large areas that divide the earth's crust. These plates float on the semi-molten rocks below them.

privatizing transferring state-owned businesses to the private sector

ration shop a store with goods to be distributed at controlled prices

raw materials a primary or partly processed product that is the basis of the finished item

recharged replaced or re-supplied

"red tape" paperwork and administration

Richter Scale the measure of the strength of an earthquake

secondary employment jobs in manufacturing industry

small-scale using few people and resources to produce something

sorghum a grain food crop

Structural Adjustment Plan (SAP) condition of a loan from IMF

subsidies a governmental supplement to keep prices artificially low

tariffs duties or taxes to be paid on imports and exports

tax breaks a form of encouragement to businesses

tertiary employment jobs in the service sector, such as in administration

toddy a drink made from palm tree juice

trade barriers laws that control what can be brought in and out of a country

underground water water below the water table

urban bias actions favoring a city, such as when cities have more favorable rates of pay

water table the level underground at which the ground is saturated with water

Index

Bold type refers to terms included in the glossary.

ACTIONAID 36, 48–49
Adivasi people 34–35
aid 48–49
agriculture 26–35, 55
appropriate technology 39
Asian Tigers 54, 59

Bangalore 20, 24–25, 42–43, 59
Bangladesh 11
Bay of Bengal 4, 11, 12
Bihar 38–39
birth rate 16–18, 21
Bhopal disaster 22
Brahmins 7
British, the 8–9, 24, 38, 56
Buddhism 6–7, 53

cash crops 26–27, 30–35
caste 6–7
children 16–17
Chipko environmental movement 48
Christian 6–7, 47
cities 22–23
climate 10–11, 26–27, 34
colony 8, 44
computer industry 25, 41, 42–43, 59
Congress Party 53
cyclones 11

death rate 16–17, 21
deforestation 56–57
Delhi 22, 52
democracy 47, 52–53, 58

demographic transition 17
development 18–19, 36–38, 40, 46–49, 52–53, 56–57
diet 27

earthquakes 14–15
economy 36–43, 46, 50–51, 54–55, 59
education 9, 16, 30, 42, 46, 56
electronics industry 25
employment 40–43, 47, 50
environment 30, 37, 44–45, 48, 49
erosion 12–13, 30, 57
exports 9, 50–52, 54–55
external debt 51, 56

family planning 16
farming 26–35, 50

Index, *continued*

film industry 39
flooding 10–11, 13, 57
fold mountains 15
food crops 26–27, 32–33
foreign investment 40–41
future 54–55, 56, 58–59

Gandhi, Indira 7
Gandhi, Mohandas 9, 39
Ganges River (Ganges Delta) 4–5, 10–11, 12–13, 56
Goa 44–45
government 38, 42, 46–47, 52–53, 58
Green Revolution, 28–29, 38
Gross Domestic Product 41, 50
Gross National Product 6, 36–37

health care 36–37
high-tech industry 10, 40–43, 59
Himalayas 4–5, 6, 10, 12–13, 15, 26, 57
Hindi 6, 39
Hinduism 6–7, 53
Hindus 47, 56
history 8, 56

Indira Gandhi Canal 30–31
independence 9, 53, 56
industry 25, 38–43, 50–51
inequality 37
Infant Mortality Rate 30, 36–37, 47, 53
imports 9, 50–51, 55
international companies 40–43, 50
International Monetary Fund (IMF) 48, 51
irrigation 26, 28–29, 30–31, 49, 56
Islam 6, 53

Kanchenjunga 4
Karnataka state 24–25, 26, 32, 42–43
Kerala 26, 46–47

languages 6
Latur 14
life expectancy 18, 37, 47, 53
literacy 30, 37, 46–47, 53

medicine 19
monsoon rains 10–11, 26–27
Mother Teresa 37
migration 20–21
migrations (animal) 30
Mumbai (Bombay) 11, 22, 23, 37, 39, 43
Muslims 7, 47, 56

Narmada River project 49
nationalized industry 38
Nehru, Jawaharlal 38
Newly Industrialized Countries (NICS) 54–55
Nilgiri Hills 26, 32–33, 34–35

Pakistan 5, 56
people, 6–7
physical geography 4, 46
plantations 27, 34–35
plates 15
pollution 13, 22, 29, 42
population 12, 16–19, 20, 24, 29, 46–47, 56
poverty 24, 36–37, 51, 53, 56
Punjab, the 8, 26, 28, 47

railroads 38, 57
rainfall 10–11
rainforest 34
religion 6–7, 12, 56

rice 26–27
Richter Scale 14–15
roads 38, 57
rural development 26–27
rural-urban migration 20–22, 56

Sardar Sarovar Dam 49
Sikhism 6
Siraj-ud-Daula 9
steel industry 38–39, 51
Structural Adjustment Plan 51

Taj Mahal 6
tea 27, 34–35
Thar Desert 4–5, 30–31, 59
tourism 44–45, 58
trade 38, 54–55
transportation 54, 57

urbanization 20–25, 50
URMUL Trust 31, 48
U.S. aid 49

water supply 11, 29, 31, 37, 56
wildlife 33

yoga 19